# Beneath
# the
# Paint

*May you never be painted in enemy territory!*

*Nancy*

# Beneath
# the
# Paint

by

Nancy Cadle Craddock

For Ron Craddock,
a man who keeps his word.

A helicopter or airplane
is said to be <u>painted</u>
when spotted over enemy lines.

# CHAPTER 1

I was fourteen the day the world changed. A decade later, two things remain the same.

1. No one saw Lee Harvey Oswald shoot President Kennedy.

2. No one saw me shoot my best friend, Ryan Thompson.

It is still hard to believe that I, Harley Ocean Hamilton, know the truth of both events.

President Kennedy, I'd only seen in magazines. Oswald, I barely knew. Ryan Thompson, that was different. He was like a brother to me.

Up until *that* November, the one of 1963, I was probably the most unlikely kid in Dallas to be tangled-up in a national event, much less the death of a president. I was barely fifteen at the time. Worse, I was in the middle of my own trial for Ryan Thompson's death.

Even today, few would expect me to know much about anything. I'd venture to say that according to the general population of Dallas, I'm still the poor, raised-by-a-single-mom kid who creates problems, not solve them.

1

During the night, a fly made its way into the courtroom. It wasn't there yesterday, that's for sure. I would have noticed. Flies and ants took my mind away from words like "intentionally," "cold-blooded" or the one I hate the most, the one that tears me up inside - "murderer".

I keep waiting for Ryan to show up. Sometimes, I can feel the warmth of his arm thrown carelessly around my shoulder. Then a cough, chair squeak or bang of a gavel jolts me back and I realize the warmth is only the afternoon sunlight streaming through the murky windows. My heart sinks as darkness swallows me again.

As the ceiling fan screeches overhead, it feels like *the* gun went off a million years ago and yet, when the prosecutor holds up a photo of Ryan, it seems like yesterday.

\*\*\*

*Is that thing loaded? Ryan asked early one spring day.*

*"Of course it is. Never seen nobody bring down a squirrel or rabbit firing nothin' but blanks," I answered with a laugh.*

*"Watch where you're pointing that thing, Harley. I'm not aiming for this to be my last day. Ain't huntin'*

season either."

"Then you'd better duck if'n I fire," I said with a smile. "Besides, I reckon its huntin' season when I say so."

Just then I heard the crackling of twigs and dry leaves on the creek bank behind me. When I turned to look, my foot slipped on a mossy rock.

All I remember after that was the slap of a body hitting the water in the shallow creek below.

It was sound I'd hear for the rest of my life.

# CHAPTER 2

As I swatted the fly circling my head, Ray Paul, my two-bit lawyer, elbowed me in the ribs hard enough to make me stop. I wanted to elbow him and his old plaid suit right back. My elbows stayed put. I was a lot of things but I wasn't a fool.

Mama said Ray Paul was the best lawyer money could buy, but I doubted it. I mean, what's the chance the *World's Best Lawyer* would choose to live on the wrong-side-of-town in a roach-infested, run-down house... and on the outskirts of humid old Dallas?

Suspenders, dandruff and an often unzipped fly, that was Ray Paul.

One thing for sure, Ray Paul was determined to make me sit still - perfectly still. That sure ain't easy in a sweltering courtroom, especially when you're all dressed-up. My new shirts were scratchy. Clothes that fit one day felt too big the next. To make matters worse, Ray Paul insisted I wear a tie which I'd never done before in my life.

I wasn't a front row kind of kid – school or church. So, sitting at the defense table with the whole city of Dallas clucking their tongues and staring holes through the back of my head was tough enough.

Every time Ray Paul yelled "Objection,

your Honor" or the judge motioned for him to approach the bench, I'd turn around to take a look. I was always searching for Mama's face or looking for a smile from Tabatha Baker, the prettiest sixth grader for miles around. I usually found them both, but neither was ever smiling, much less sending me a wave or a wink.

Once, I accidentally caught the eye of Mrs. Thompson, Ryan's mom. Without thinking, I nodded and smiled, remembering times she invited me to spend the night so Ryan and I could get up early to go fishing. Mornings, we'd slip out as quietly as we could. If not, we'd get stuck with Billy, Ryan's younger brother, and our day would be ruined.

I wanted to escape the anger in her eyes but I couldn't. There wasn't any place to run to, and besides, I'd run once and that was part of my problem. Yes, Ray Paul was at a disadvantage. Even I knew that.

As Prosecutor Ed White thundered on about my shortcomings, I chanced another quick glance over my shoulder. Mrs. Thompson glared at me and mouthed "I hate you". Her words came as a shock. I whirled back around and bit my lip.

It was only her grief-talking I told myself, trying not to cry.

To steady my nerves, I forced my mind to go blank and followed the path of the fly, trying not to think any farther than the tip of its wings.

Even though I'd been locked up at the county jail for almost a year waiting for my trial, it still felt too weird being there to get much rest. Policemen were in and out at all hours, and things didn't quiet down until the wee hours of the morning. On top of it all, my stomach always ached, making it nearly impossible to sleep anyway.

Unfortunately, Ray Paul didn't like me slouching any better than twisting or turning, or shooing away flies. He let that be known by a kick or two under the table. Nothing that anyone could see, mind you – just enough to bring me upright in my chair.

During a lunch break, I overhead Mama say to him, "Harley is doing as well as any other fourteen-year-old around."

"Well, that's just the point, isn't it? He's not any other fourteen-year-old. He's on trial for m-u-r-d-e-r, Mrs. Hamilton. And whether you like it or not, I don't plan to go down with him. I've got a reputation to protect," Ray Paul answered as he slung his suit jacket on the conference table.

"And I've got a boy to protect, Mr. Big Shot Lawyer," Mama replied as she narrowed her eyes.

Ray Paul pulled on his frayed red suspenders. "Just remember, they're trying him as an adult. We're looking at twenty-to-life for your boy, l-a-d-y."

Mama didn't answer.

7

Ray Paul pulled on his suspenders again. When he let go, they popped against his chest and dandruff sprinkled down, settling on his shoulders.

Yes, we were all pretty much on edge. And even though I didn't think it was possible for things to get worse between Mama and Ray Paul, they did. The closer our turn came to tell what happened *that* day, the worse they bickered. I guess the real trouble was the other side had a dead body, and our side didn't have one shred of evidence that the whole thing was an accident, except my word, and no one acted like that was worth hearing.

***

*"We're gonna get caught, as sure as anything,"* Ryan said as he watched me sling things right-and-left in the back bedroom closet where Mama still kept some of Dad's old things.*

*"WE? What do you mean WE? So far it's only ME! Get over here and help me. How's about pushing these old coats out of my way so I can get my hand on some shells?"*

*"Harley, I don't know. We've done some dumb things before but this is probably going to be right up there with jumping in Jimmie Pearl's pond on Christmas Eve. Scaring her half to death, I might add."*

*"The look on her face was worth it all. Thought for sure she was going to hit us over the head with her Bible."* I

burst out laughing as I kicked a pile of old sweaters and a flat football to the other side of the closet.

Ryan slid an old Halloween outfit and some empty hangers across the closet bar, out of my face. "Figured Jimmie Pearl would call our parents to come fetch us but she didn't. Heck, you had her laying out a spread of cookies and hot chocolate before our clothes were dry. I swear you could talk your way out of almost anything."

"Bingo." I pulled the rifle out and laid it on the bed along with a box of shells. "Let's go."

"Harley, are you sure? This whole thing is bound to get us in a heap of trouble."

"Stop with all this 'we' stuff. So far, all you've done is watch me shove old clothes around," I answered with a laugh. "Well, are you coming or not?"

"I guess so. Just remember, this convoluted thing is your idea."

"What kind of a word is that - convoluted?" I asked with a hearty laugh.

"The heck if I know," Ryan answered, laughing along with me. "Just something I heard my uncle say after the Rose Bowl last year."

"Well, this ain't the Rose Bowl. Come on. Hurry up. We gotta get goin' or the day's gonna be wasted. Besides, you'll thank me in the end," I said as we headed out the door.

As it turned out, nothing could be further from the truth.

***

"If it seems like I'm on a mission. I AM. Yes, sir, I want everyone... all of us... to leave here knowing the TRUTH, ladies and gentlemen. The TRUTH. We're not here to GOSSIP about it. We're not here to be FRIGHTENED by it. We just want to go away from here carrying the plain old simple TRUTH about that day with us." Ed White said each sentence louder than the one before it.

Ray Paul pulled a worn-out looking toothpick from his mouth and jumped to his feet. "Objection, your Honor. The defense isn't here to HIDE the truth. We, too, want to lay the truth at the feet of the court. Judge, I beg you, he's making it sound like we don't want the truth, but in reality..."

"Objection overruled," the judge cut in with a scowl.

I wondered if Ray Paul was making sense to anyone other than himself. *Feet of the court. Good grief.* I wondered if he meant "At the feet of Lady Justice" but I'd never know for sure. What I *did* know is Ray Paul talked as weird as he dressed. Still, he was the lawyer, whereas, I was the cold-blooded criminal - at least, according to almost everyone I'd ever known in the fourteen years I'd been on the face-of-the-earth. That much was evident from the whispers that swirled around me during the days police were still questioning me, and I was still free to come-and-go. In some ways, it was a relief Mama couldn't come up with bail money and I was shoved in a cramped little cell. At least, I was away from the prying eyes and clucking tongues of Dallas.

Ed White's forceful tone brought me back as he thundered, "It may be a hard truth, that's for sure, but just knowing the truth is a whole lot better... ladies and gentlemen... than forever trying to get to the bottom of a lie."

I wouldn't have been surprised to hear a few "amens" when Ed White pointed a finger at me. But the jurors sat still, only their heads nodding. For a split second, I nearly burst out laughing looking at those bobbing-head human dolls. As usual, a swift kick from Ray Paul brought me back to the seriousness of my situation.

"The truth, and nothing but the truth, that's all we're asking here," Ed White said as he lowered himself back in his chair.

Before his bottom had time to settle there, Ray Paul sprung up and shouted, "Objection, your Honor."

"Honestly! Again, OVERRULED! For Pete's sake, it's an opening statement, Ray Paul," the judge bellowed. "He can say what he wants. Now, sit yourself down and stay there."

"But... your Honor... he's making it sound like only the prosecution is interested in seeking the truth. I can assure you - my client, Harley Hamilton is just as concerned with the truth as the prosecution. Maybe... even more so. I dare say we have reason to be more concerned than anyone here today. Seems only fair that everyone knows it. Besides, how much longer is his opening statement gonna last? We've been at this for days."

"You'll have your turn," the judge answered, running his handkerchief across his forehead. "Didn't they explain what opening statements are in law school?"

Ray Paul's only comeback was "Yes, your Honor." Then, he shuffled some papers and muttered, "And the long-winded ones usually flunked-out."

I nodded but said nothing. Ray Paul's words were definitely worth a laugh but my ankles already hurt, and I didn't want to run the risk of another swift kick.

That's about as much as we covered that day or maybe they talked longer. I don't know. I didn't pay all that much attention. My mind kept drifting back to better times, back before my best friend died on the rocky bottom of Muddy Creek - with a bullet in his head.

# CHAPTER 3

Mama and I left Galveston back in fifty-three and headed toward Dallas when I was only four-years-old. Mama said she needed a change from all that gritty-gray sand and wanted to live where odor of fish didn't hang the air. At the time, I was too young to know she was also fleeing from bad times - and Daddy.

I've tried to remember moving to Dallas and when I first met Ryan. The truth is I don't rightly know. Even though we were in the same first grade class, my earliest memory of him is sometime around the end of second grade.

After recess one spring day, Mrs. Warner stood chatting with another teacher while pudgy Wilbur Cunningham was hogging all the water from the fountain. Water dribbled clear to his chin while the rest of us sweated in line, desperately waiting our turn at the metal cooler.

As sweat trickled down my forehead, I decided to give Wilbur a reason to hurry along. After considering a punch, a pinch or a kick, I settled on a kick, figuring it wouldn't be as noticeable as the other two.

I wasn't much of a kick, but I should have known he'd make the most of it. Through jerky sobs, he cried out, "Harley kicked me."

Mrs. Warner grabbed me by the shoulder

and yanked me to her. "Harley, did you kick Wilbur? Because if you did, you're going to stand in the corner for the rest of the afternoon. I'm sick-and-tired of you causing chaos in my classroom."

Before I had time to answer, a voice further down the line sung out. "Harley didn't do it. It was me, me - not Harley."

Astonished, I whirled around to see Ryan moving steadily toward Mrs. Warner and me.

Mrs. Warner's eyes opened wide. "Well, I do declare. Ryan, are you sure? I've never known you to do such a thing,"

"Yes, ma'am, it was me. Wilbur was holding up the line," Ryan replied.

"Ryan, tell Wilbur you're sorry and get back in line. No water for you, Harley, and you can just head on back to the classroom."

"But, Mrs. Warner, I didn't do nothin'," I protested.

"You heard me. Now!"

"Not fair," I whispered as I walked away smiling. Finding a friend was worth a heap more than any old sip of water.

From that moment on, Ryan was my best friend. I mean how many people are willing to take the blame for something they didn't do, just to keep someone else out of trouble?

Yes, being friends with Ryan was almost like having a brother. In fact, it was the best part of living in Dallas – or maybe anywhere.

14

# CHAPTER 4

Ed White pointed a slim manicured finger straight at me. "What we have here is not an accident. No, what we have here is a crime - pure and simple. A crime. And how do we know that? I'll tell you how. We know that because once the gun went off and poor Ryan's body was thrown to the water below, we have no evidence - not one shred, that Harley Hamilton tried to save him."

It was yet another day of opening statements and I must have been slouching because Ray Paul gave me another swift kick under the table. Immediately, I straightened my shoulders and sat up straight. I can't say that I blame Ray Paul for his constant kicks and occasional pinch. My word was all he had. Not much for any lawyer to work with, considering it was a murder trial.

I wanted to kick myself. Couldn't just go and get myself in a little trouble – shoplifting, trespassing, or something like that. No, I had to be a big shot and mess around with a gun, and a loaded one at that. Whatever was I thinking? One thing for sure, I'd never be so foolhardy again. Considering the outcome of my actions, it wasn't hard to understand why the whole town wanted to lock me up. What they didn't know was going to jail... or a juvenile home... whatever it was called, was all the same to me. I'd be where Ryan would never be again... among the living.

I held my body up straight next to Ray Paul but let my mind wander back a couple of years to the fourth grade field trip. Bits of conversation flitted through my mind like the annoying fly that kept landing on my head.

"Well, if this ain't living, I don't know what is," Ryan shouted as we climbed on the chartered bus bound for the outskirts of Fort Worth.

"You got that right," I answered.

I never imagined I'd be making the trip but I was boarding the bus with the rest of my class. To tell the truth, I didn't care where we were going. It didn't make any difference to me if it was a horse farm in Fort Worth or just around the corner. It felt good just to be like everyone else. It was a miracle that I was on the bus in the first place.

The day I handed Mama the permission form, she sat down, clearly distressed. "Harley, I don't know. I'll see what I can do. Ten dollars is a pretty big chunk of my paycheck and "tipping the waitress" is something, believe it or not, big-city-Dallas-folks don't seem to know nothin' about."

"I know Mama, but I really want to go. Everyone's going. It's not a regular old school bus and we're going to have box lunches and everything. Don't you want me go?"

"Harley, it's not that I *don't* want you to go, it's just that things are a really tight right now. Rent's due in a week and I've still got to pay the doctor for the strep throat you had after jumping in Jimmie Pearl's pond last month - the middle of December, I might add!"

"Sorry. Heck if I know what made me do such a crazy thing. I'm sorry, really I am."

"That's just it, Harley, I've told you thousands of times, you've got to think before you act."

I sat down at the table across from Mama. "I workin' on it, really I am."

Mama smiled. "I know." Biting her bottom lip, she continued, "As much as I hate to do it, maybe I can borrow some money from Grandmother Hamilton."

"Do... do... do you think she'll know wh... wh... where Dad is?" I stammered. A glimmer of hope worked its way from my toes up.

"We've been through this a million times. You know your dad is a free spirit, but I'm sure he thinks about you more than you could ever know."

"That's not the same. Heck, I haven't seen him for more than two years and even then, it was only for a couple of hours."

"Yes, but if I remember right, you two packed a lot of fun into those two hours," Mama answered with a faraway look on her face, as if remembering better days with dad.

Determined to get my point across, I said, "Mama, it's not the same. I mean... look at Mr. Thompson. Hardly an evening goes by that he

17

isn't outside playing ball with Ryan and Billy. I want a dad like that. I want a dad that plays ball with me."

"Harley, you know the Thompsons always include you. Now, isn't that nice of them?" Mama answered a tad louder.

"It's not the same and you know it," I replied in an ever louder voice.

"That's about enough, Harley. I won't have you talking to me like that. Whether you like it or not, I'm all you've got and that's the end of it."

"What am I suppose to do – pretend I've got a dad like the rest of the world?"

"Look, if it will make you feel any better, I'll ask Grandmother Hamilton if she's heard from him lately. You just never know, your dad might swing by here any day."

I stood and gave my chair a hard shove under the table, making the plastic salt and pepper shakers rattle as they teetered back-and-forth. "Well, I'm not holding my breath. Wouldn't you know I'd be the one to get stuck with a dad like that!"

"That's enough, Harley. Enough!"

I knew when to stop pushing Mama. I'd said all I could and figured I might as well give up thinking about everything - field trips and dad. If wishing about a thing made it come true, I'd be Ryan. Well, minus his annoying little brother, that is.

# CHAPTER 5

"I had forgotten about the gun. It belonged to my husband… my ex-husband, that is," Mama said as Ray Paul paced around what passed for a conference room on the first floor of the Dallas jail. Despite the fact it was late and we'd been sitting in court all day, Ray Paul kept firing questions left-and-right at Mama.

"And where exactly was the gun in the first place?" Ray Paul questioned.

"In the spare bedroom closet. Well, not really a bedroom. It's just kind of a storage area. The landlord likes to call it a third bedroom so that he can up the rent."

"That's more information than the jury needs to know. Let's keep it as bedroom, shall we? Besides, a 'bedroom closet' will play more dignified in court than some kind of storage area."

Mama put both elbows on the long conference table and rested her head in her hands.

"Let's start again." Ray Paul cleared his throat. Keeping his eyes on something out the window, he asked again, "Where did the gun come from, Mrs. Hamilton?"

"It belonged to my ex-husband. He used to cart it with him everywhere he went," Mama said with a frown as she added under her breath, "along with one pretty girl after another."

"I hope you didn't say what I thought you said. The jury sure doesn't need to know about any of that!" Ray Paul said as he whirled around toward Mama.

"Sorry, couldn't help myself."

"Well, talk like that is definitely not going to help Harley. Now, let's get on with it…. ummm… oh, yes… where was the gun kept?"

"Behind winter clothes and what-nots in the back bedroom closet," Mama answered, looking pleased.

"Whoa! BEHIND clothes makes Harley sound sneaky," Ray Paul said with a frown.

Mama glared at me as she answered. "Well, he was!"

"That may be, but I hardly think telling the jury that your kid is sneaky is going to do you - or him, an ounce of good. Honestly, whose side are you on?" Ray Paul questioned as he ran his fingers through his stringy yellow hair.

"I didn't say Harley was sneaky. Taking the gun was sneaky… but you're right. I know I can do better."

"Alright, let's try again. Now, ummm… okay then… Mrs. Hamilton, where was the gun kept?"

"In the back bedroom closet."

"Good job. That's all the jury needs to know. We want to give them information on a "need-to-know" basis."

"I understand."

"And the ammunition?" Ray Paul asked.

"In the same closet as the gun," Mama

answered.

"Remember. We're not going to hand them anything we don't have to give them. Just say in the spare bedroom closet."

"Oh, good grief." Mama stood up. "I just told them that the gun was in the closet. It's not like we have closets here, closets there, and closets everywhere. Besides, the jury isn't stupid, you know," Mama said with a flash of anger in her eyes.

"Maybe they are, and maybe they aren't. You never know. We want to let THEM do the dotting of the i's and crossing of the t's. Some juries do and some juries don't."

"I'm not a lawyer, but it seems like they're going to know that Harley put the bullets in the gun. Doesn't take a genius to figure that one out," Mama said, reaching for her purse.

"Speaking of money, Mrs. Hamilton, my records show you're behind in your payment and we haven't really even gotten started yet."

"We weren't speaking of "money" and I told you I've got some coming from relatives. Don't worry Ray Paul, you'll get what's coming to you." Mama bent down and kissed my cheek. "Bye, Sweetie. I'll be back after work tomorrow."

And with a bang of the door, she was gone.

Ray Paul followed, trotting behind Mama and I was escorted by a guard back up to my cell on the fifth floor.

# CHAPTER 6

Money. More often than not, there wasn't enough. As usual, Grandma Hamilton didn't come through for the field trip. Not that I could blame her. Why would she feel bound to fork her badly needed Social Security money to a kid she hardly knew?

Luckily, it all worked out. Whenever Mama needed extra money, she rearranged her schedule at *The Lone Star Diner*, her regular job, so that she could waitress Friday and Saturday night over at the *Carousel Club*. Mama also wrangled a promise out of the owner, Jack Ruby, that I could tag along with her. That way, I wouldn't be left home alone until the wee hours of the morning.

I was probably somewhere around nine or ten when Mama first started working there. In the beginning, Mama made me spend evenings sitting on a chair facing the back wall. That way, I couldn't see the girls on stage.

I protested, "Good grief. It's so smoky in there, I couldn't see anything if I tried."

Mama frowned. "Well, when the lights come up and the smoke clears, I expect to see progress on those buffalos and owls and whatever else you're always sketching."

After so many evenings, my buffalos and owls were plum-near-perfect and Mama gave in and said, "I don't want people thinking you're a dead body, so I reckon there'd be no harm if you move every now and then... but no gawking at the working girls."

"I won't gawk. I promise."

"Well, alright then."

Not long after that, Mr. Ruby said I could bus tables. He told Thelma, the cashier, to pay me a dollar and a half at the end of every evening!

Having something-to-do made a huge difference, and it got so I looked forward to the evenings that Mama worked there. Clearing off tables was a breeze. The only thing they served besides liquor was pizza. And like everything else, in no time at all, I was eating my share of it with Bernie, the cook.

All of that was great, but the part that I liked best was taking care of Mr. Ruby's dogs. He had five and always brought a couple with him to the *Carousel*. I'd take them out back whenever they needed to stretch their legs or do their business. A couple of Saturdays, Mr. Ruby had me walk one dog home to his apartment and bring another dog back. In fact, it got so when I wasn't clearing off a table, I was walking a dog or eating pizza. Crisp dollars and shiny half-dollars were adding up, to boot!

Since Mama and me were renters, we didn't get to have pets. So, I pretended Jack Ruby's dogs were mine and wondered if any of the *Carousel* patrons thought they belonged to me. I hoped so.

I wouldn't say Mr. Ruby was like a dad, or

anything like that, but it was the *Carousel* money that got me on the bus bound for Ft. Worth with the rest of my class. From the moment I stepped on board, I knew walking a dog through a dark alley at night or wiping up runny pizza sauce in a smoke-filled room was worth it.

For the field trip, everyone had to choose a partner. As soon as Ryan and I plopped down in our seat and the bus left the curb, I pulled out a pack of cards. No one else had thought to bring anything, so everyone ended up watching the two of us play. I felt special knowing that everyone else knew that I, poor old Harley Hamilton, was Ryan Thompson's field trip buddy. I really didn't care whether I won or lost some old card game. I'd already won.

It was hard to imagine any two people more different than Ryan and me. He lived in a really nice house and came from a neighborhood where sprinklers whirled atop bright green grass. It was a neighborhood where sleek cars glided down paved driveways at the end of every day. Most of all, it was a place where dads spent time teaching their kids how scores were kept and games were played. And it showed. Ryan and others like him were the good ball players. They were the ones who always picked the teams and decided whether the rest of us would or wouldn't play.

I'd like to think I might have been a good ball player had anyone taken the time to work with me. But no one did. Even though Mama was one to throw a shoe at me every now and then, she wasn't much on tossing a ball around for fun.

Besides, patches of dirt showed through the dusty grass that surrounded our house - the one with the peeling paint. And the only cars that appeared in our pebbly driveway were faded-out clunkers driven by men hoping to get more from Mama than a peck on the cheek after some movie or cheap date.

The bangs of my dirty brown hair were always crooked whereas Ryan's blonde ones were perfectly straight – always. Nor did they ever dip or hang sideways.

Even Ryan's pearly white teeth were straight. Mine were crooked, dull and ordinary.

Most of all, there was the issue of our Christian names. I mean how could the name Harley Ocean Hamilton even begin to compete with Ryan Duane Thompson? Who in their right mind would choose "Harley" when they could have a name like "Ryan"?

Ryan sounded perfect - normal. It wasn't a name you got because your dad rode a motorcycle or because as your mama said "You started out as a gleam in your daddy's eye late one night on a deserted beach". Who had a name like mine? No one important, that's for sure. Certainly no one I'd ever heard of in the entire city of Dallas... make that in the entire Lone Star State!

Worse still, Ryan never cursed.

I did.

All in all, it was darn hard not to be envious of Ryan – who he was, what he did, and all that he had - right down to the constant parade of shiny new bicycles that grew taller when he did. No one seemed to care that I'd been peddling around on a much too small, rusted-out old bike for way too long.

Even though Ryan had been dead over a year now, it never ceased to amaze me that he chose to be a friend with ordinary old me. For sure, if we hadn't been best friends, we would have been great enemies.

I doubted anyone on the jury would believe the good part about me and do-away with the bad so I kept my thoughts to myself.

# CHAPTER 7

"Ladies and gentlemen of the jury," Ed White shouted as he walked across the room and pointed a finger in my general direction, "it's no big secret. This was a crime committed for several different reasons. The first is pure old jealousy - nothing more, nothing less. That's right - jealousy. And when we examine the differences, it's not so hard to understand. Not really."

"Having a *week* of opening statements is what's hard to understand," Ray Paul muttered to himself, more than to me, but I heard it just the same. I gave Ray Paul a little "thumbs-up". *Maybe there was hope for him, yet.*

Ed White's pointed finger at my face would have challenged my determination not to cry, but heck, I'd already cried my eyes out. My tears flowed like a fountain when the sheriff tugged on a metal zipper until thick black plastic completely covered Ryan's face. They continued falling as I drug home my dad's old gun while police were hovering around Ryan's dead body. And now, almost a year and a half later, the tears were still there - under the surface maybe, but there just the same. Most days, it took a lot of effort to keep them from spilling-out and running down my face.

Ed White hadn't been there to see my tears, so I really couldn't feel badly toward him for makin' me out as some kind of a mean-hearted, hateful person who would go and shoot his best friend. And even though it wasn't quite like that, the end result was the same.

Ed White sounded smart, but he didn't know everything. For one thing, he didn't know about my good hearing.

On an overcast night when clouds hold sound down, I can hear the lonely sound of the midnight train several miles from the Dallas jail. I don't mean just the train, I hear the clackety-clack as the boxcars roll over the ties - one by one. Back home, I can hear the neighbor's dog whining to go out, and I always hear Mama's soft cries in her sleep. All three never fail to make me feel sad.

When I was younger, I could hear my dad's motorcycle before it came into sight. There were other motorcycles up and down Tex Avenue but Mama said she always knew when Dad was about a mile or two from the house. I would run toward the door with a smile on my face.

Once there, I wouldn't budge until his chopper came into view, even if it meant I was kept waiting while he stopped for cigarettes along the way.

As I got older, the waiting was harder. And now, it seemed like my life was nothing but waiting. During the day, I marked time by the number of recesses the court took. We got a fifteen minute break before lunch and another one every afternoon around three o'clock.

Somewhere in the middle, we had an hour off for lunch. After the last recess one day early in November, a new face was summoned to the front of the courtroom.

"Your honor, the People call Delbert Cunningham to the stand," Ed White said with a smile as he looked toward the back of the room.

The guard swung open the door and a skinny, nervous-looking man trotted down the aisle to where we all sat. My eyes followed the man's every movement as he placed his hand on the Bible and promised to tell nothing but the truth - the whole truth, nothin' but the truth.

"Please state your name for the record," the judge said.

"Delbert Cunningham. Ain't got no middle name. Never did."

"Proceed," the judge replied, with a nod to Ed White.

Ed White smiled toward this Cunningham man as if the two of them were the best of friends... and maybe they were.

"Your place of business?"

"I'm the owner of Cunningham's Chopper Shop."

"Is your cycle shop located here in Dallas, Mr. Cunningham?"

The man tugged at the collar of his shirt before answering. "Yep. Near the corner of Third and Main."

"And how is it that you came to know the

accused, Harley Ocean Hamilton?" Ed White thumbed through the pages of a long, white legal pad.

"I knowed his daddy. He used to come by my shop every so often… but I don't know the exact dates or nothin' like that."

"That's quite okay."

Ed White shuffled through a several pages in his legal pad before asking, "What kind of a man would you say Daniel Hamilton, father of accused Harley Hamilton, seems to be? After all, you've had dealings with him, isn't that right?"

Ray Paul sprang out from behind the table where we sat. "Objection, your Honor. Totally irrelevant. This case isn't about the boy's father."

"Overruled. Background information." the judge said, louder than usual. "Continue."

"But your Honor," Ray Paul implored.

"Goes to character." The judge nodded for Ed White to continue.

Ed White cleared his throat. "As I was saying… what kind of a man would you judge Harley Hamilton's father to be?"

"Fine. Far as I knows. He only came 'round every now and then, usually looking to buy some spare parts or fix a flat on his chopper," Delbert Cunningham answered.

"And did he pay?"

"Fair and square, same as all the rest."

"Well, can you tell us then, what others say about him? Remember that you're under oath here today," Ed White replied.

Ray Paul jumped up. "Objection, your Honor. The witness is aware of the oath he just took. He doesn't need the *esteemed* Mr. White to remind him."

"Overruled and by the way, Ray Paul, you might want to remember that Mr. Cunningham is *not* a witness for your side."

Ed White laughed.

Ray Paul slunk back down.

Ed White then moved closer to Delbert Cunningham and said again, "What do others say about Daniel Hamilton?"

At this point, sweat began to glisten on Delbert Cunningham's forehead. I glanced back at Mama. She had a puzzled look on her face which worried me.

Ray Paul bent his head and whispered in my ear, "No outburst, young man, no matter what. Understand?"

I whispered, "He'd better not say nothin' bad 'bout my dad."

"Well… ahhh… well… ahhh," Delbert Cunningham stammered, looking down at his hands.

Still, he didn't answer. I could feel most everyone leaning forward behind me, shifting to sit on the edge of their chair. Still, no answer.

Finally, the judge lost his patience and thundered, "For the love of God, man, spit it out."

"A one-percenter. There's some that say he's a one-percenter."

"Objection, your Honor... I think," Ray Paul said looking confused. "At least I think I object, your Honor. Hearsay, for sure."

Even the judge looked puzzled. "Well, before I know whether it's sustained or overruled, I've got to know what he's talking about. Approach the bench, gentlemen."

As both lawyers walked toward the front of the room, the judge fished around with his fingers in a water pitcher for ice cubes. After pulling out a couple, he dropped them in his glass of water and motioned the men closer.

Ed White moved swiftly toward the judge. Ray Paul shuffled up beside Ed White. As the three whispered back-and-forth, their heads bobbed up and down.

Even with my good hearing, I only caught a phrase every so often, nothing that made any sense.

After a couple of minutes, Ed White turned and walked back toward Delbert Cunningham.

Ray Paul sat down and slung his arm around my shoulder. "Don't worry about what he says. Besides, his testimony isn't gonna matter all that much in the end."

I made a fist with my right hand and stared straight ahead.

"Now, Mr. Cunningham, would you please tell the jury here, what being a one-percenter means," Ed White asked, with a smile on his face.

"Well... ahhh... well... ahhh... it's been estimated one-percent of all motorcycle riders are hoodlums – up to no good...evil."

In a matter of seconds, Ed Paul was back on his feet, shouting. "Motion to strike! How pertinent could someone's opinion about Harley's father be? And who even knows if what this Cunningham is telling is right anyway. Who figured the statics on this? For this to even be admissible, we need studies, reports, that kind-of-thing."

The judge nodded. "Clerk, kindly strike from the record that Mr. Hamilton is a one-percenter."

Still standing, Ray Paul exclaimed, "But judge, the jury has already heard it."

The judge turned toward the jury and said, "The jury will dismiss what the witness just said and all this nonsense about one-percent."

Still not looking pleased, Ray Paul said, "But... but... they already heard it... and this could subconsciously affect their decision toward my client. I call for an immediate mistrial!"

"Save it for appeal, Ray Paul," the judge answered as he took a swig of ice-water. "Let's continue. Your turn, Ray Paul, do you want it or not?"

"Yes, your Honor," Ray Paul answered as Delbert Cunningham wiped his forehead with the back of his hand. "Now... Mr. Cunningham... it seems to me that people can say anything they darn-near please, any time they want. Would you agree to that?"

"I reckon so."

"Well… then… I guess the question is what do you say? Do you have any reason to believe that Daniel Hamilton was part of any organized motorcycle crime group? Wait. Let me rephrase that. Do you, yourself, believe that Daniel Hamilton was up to no-good or was a trouble-maker?" Ray Paul asked, looking straight at Delbert Cunningham's face.

After a long pause, Mr. Cunningham said, "No, sir, I don't. He seemed like an okay sort of person to me. A down-on-your-luck kind of guy, but that's about it."

"Thank you, Mr. Cunningham. No more questions. Your Honor, the defense reserves the right to recall this witness at a later date, if needed."

"So noted," the judge answered with a yawn. "The witness is excused."

Delbert Cunningham rose from his chair and left the stand which seemed to end the whole thing.

As he passed my way, Ray Paul clamped his hand firmly on my arm and whispered, "Not a sound, not a peep. Harley, I'm not kidding. Understand?"

"Got it, Ray Paul and now, get your hand off of me!" I whispered back. *Down-on-your-luck kind of guy!* He made Dad sound like some down-trodden poor old soul. Well, maybe he was, and maybe he wasn't, but that shouldn't be anyone's business except for Mama's and me. I uncurled my fist. One thing for sure, Dad wasn't at Muddy Creek *that* day, and he didn't deserve to be trampled on in a Dallas courtroom.

Even when Ray Paul moved his hand, I sat still - not out of fear of Ray Paul but out of respect for Mama. She wasn't the kind of person to bring up dad in front of Dallas folk any more than necessary, which was lucky for old Delbert Cunningham. He got to walk back out, the same way he came in, teeth and all.

\*\*\*

*Footsteps. The steady crunch of leaves on the ground. Stopping only when we stopped Moving when we moved. Not loud by any means, but I heard them long before Ryan and I reached the creek. Neither of us acknowledged the crunchy sound following us. What was the point? We knew he'd catch up eventually. He always did.*

*And that's why I shouldn't have been startled. But, I was. For some unknown reason, I was. If I could live that one second over again I wouldn't turn around — not for anything or anybody. I would stand perfectly still if it took the rest of my life. Maybe, then, I wouldn't have slipped and lost my grip.*

*And now this… a trial. People staring and*

37

*whispering, forever accused. Of course, why wouldn't they? After all, in their eyes, I was the kid who shot my best friend in the head with a twenty-two. Who wouldn't stare at a hoodlum like that?*

*It didn't take a jury to say that my actions were far worse than having a down-on-your luck kind of dad.*

*Even I knew that.*

***

The door squeaked shut as Delbert Cunningham exited the courtroom. Slowly, Ray Paul let go of my arm and I released the grip I had on the arm of my chair.

Outside, someone was dribbling a basketball. I tried to figure out if it was a real game by the pattern of bouncing sounds on the pavement. The longer I listened, the more certain I was that someone was walking along, giving the basketball an occasional dribble.

The ball's familiar sound took me back, away from the words of Delbert Cunningham, away from Ed White, Ray Paul, even the judge.

I melted away from the courtroom to a better time and place, a time when my arms weren't bruised, my chest wasn't tight and my stomach didn't ache. I entered a place where Ryan stood up after falling, without a hole in his head.

***

Ryan bounced a basketball as we made our way down Main Street looking in store windows and stopping to talk to familiar faces. By way of hot fudge sundaes at the Lone Star Soda Fountain, we ended up, as usual, in the back corner of the Longhorn Grocery Store.

Inside, a large banner hung from the ceiling with the words, "Books Galore." A grand name for nothing more than a couple of shelves crammed full of dusty books and worn-out magazines. Certainly nothing up-to-date. No matter. Every so often, Ryan and I would stroll through the store and spend the better part of an afternoon thumbing through comic books as the owner, Mr. Cox, glared at us from behind the cash register.

Between customers, Mr. Cox would attempt to shoo us out, saying, "Books for paying customers only."

"We might be paying customers," Ryan said with a laugh one day.

"If that's so, how's about letting me get a look at your money? That way, we'll know for sure," Mr. Cox replied.

Since I never had a cent to my name and Ryan had already spent his on our sundaes, we reluctantly put down the comic books and headed for the door.

"Hey, Ryan, tell your dad that I'll see him on the golf course Saturday morning – same as usual, depending on the weather, of course," Mr. Cox called after us.

"Sure thing," Ryan answered, as he let go of the heavy door.

"Dang it. We always have to leave before I get to the end of Superman," I muttered as I shielded my eyes from the late afternoon sun.

*Ryan switched the basketball to his other hand. "What's there to read? Superman saves the day. All of his books end the exact same way."*

*"So... I know that," I said as I knocked the basketball out from under his hand and darted away, "just be nice to see it in black and white."*

\*\*\*

A cough from a juror and Ray Paul's pencil tapping brought me back from the past. I don't know how long I was daydreaming but a lot of time must have passed because soon afterwards, the judge banged his gavel and said, "Court dismissed."

I wondered what Ryan would say if he knew I was spending all of my time in a courtroom instead of down at our favorite fishing hole or outside on a basketball court.

I looked up at Ray Paul. "Not that I care, but do you think anyone will ever pick me to play on their team again? You're a lawyer... maybe you know these things."

"I doubt it, kid. Seems to me, the way things stand now, there's not likely to be a lot of friends for you in the future. But... providing you come clean about everything... maybe there's still a chance of turning this whole thing around and redeeming yourself. What do you say?"

There wasn't anything to say. Deep in my heart, I already knew playing on a basketball team or any kind of team for that matter, was probably a privilege reserved for others - not for a kid the likes of me. As for fishing, or anything close to it, I didn't plan to be near water - ever again. So, nothing else mattered, not really.

# CHAPTER 8

It didn't take a genius to know Jack Henry, one of the guards, was hoping for a date with Mama. When no one else was around, he'd unlock my cell door and let her in. Usually, we'd sit huddled on the edge of my cot while Mama caught me up on what was happening on the outside world.

One November day, she arrived carrying a lopsided chocolate cake. "Look what I've got."

"You can feed it to the guard for all I care," I blurted out as she pulled wax paper away from gooey chocolate icing. Today her hands were so shaky, the wax paper rattled.

"Harley, what a thing to say," Mama replied as she dropped the chocolatey wax paper in the trash can. "Mr. Ruby and the girls over at the *Carousel* sent this for your birthday. Wasn't that nice of them?"

"Guess so."

"Come on, Harley, you only turn fourteen once."

"I'm sorry, Mama. It's a real pretty cake and it was sweet of them to go to all that trouble, but I'm not in any mood to celebrate this year."

"For Pete's Sake, Harley, it's your birthday. You've never turned down a piece of chocolate cake in your life," Mama replied. Her brows were furrowed and there was a deep crease between her eyes.

"I mean it, Mama, they shouldn't have gone to the trouble. I wish everyone would just forget about me."

"Things will get better, you'll see," Mother answered with a smile, although I detected a small quiver in her voice.

"How do you figure that? Nothing's going to get better. I'm alive and Ryan isn't." I threw myself down on my worn-out, lumpy cot. "It should have been me."

"What a thing to say! Look, Harley, wishing or grieving ain't gonna bring him back. So, why don't we just concentrate on the positive."

"Nothin's right," I said, turning my face to the wall.

Mama patted my head. "I can't stay long but I sure hate having to leave you like this, kiddo. I'm working a double shift. Another waitress covered for me long enough to bring the cake over, but I've gotta be headin' on back. Now, cheer up. Eat some cake. Starving won't do the trick, sweetie. Not gonna change a thing." She bent down and kissed the top of my head before calling for Jack Henry to let her out.

"Oh, and Harley, guess what?" She said in her "high-pitched, isn't this exciting" voice as she stepped out of my cell.

"What?" *Good grief, now what? Couldn't she see I was in the throes of despair!*

Mr. Ruby told me the President is going to

come to town – here, right here in little old Dallas. Isn't that exciting?"

"The President?"

"You know... Kennedy. Isn't that exciting? I can hardly wait."

"Yay, I guess," I answered, highly doubting an over-worked waitress or her delinquent son was going to get a glance at the president. Still, I smiled just to be polite. Mama face lit-up and she giggled which made me laugh.

Mama always had a way of getting me to smile on the worse of days.

As the clickety-clap of her run-down heels faded away, I burrowed under a scratchy blanket. It was hard not to think about happier times and better birthdays as rain plopped against my small window. For a brief moment, I wondered if for the rest of my life if I'd always feel this crummy whenever my birthday came around. I sure hoped not as I reached over and drug my finger through rich chocolate icing.

After I devoured a couple pieces of cake, Ray Paul showed up.

"How you doing, Harley?"

"Fine, I guess," I answered with a shrug of my shoulders.

"Good. That's good. Anything you need?"

"Nope... nothing I can think of."

"Looks like someone brought you a chocolate cake," Ray Paul said with a smile. "Your birthday?"

"Yeah," I answered with another shrug.

"Harley, I've been doing a lot of thinking about you," Ray Paul said as he leaned closer toward my cell bars, making me feel trapped.

"What about?" I asked, trying not to care.

"Well, this here… is what I think… I think you *want* to tell me something. But on the other hand, you *want* to be punished. Am I right?"

"Maybe," I answered. *Drats! Old Ray Paul must be having a light-bulb moment. Just what I didn't need on my birthday, of all days.*

"That's pretty much what I thought. Here's what I suggest - why don't you give yourself the best birthday present *ever* by coming clean about the whole thing?"

I shrugged for the third time and turned back toward my cot.

# CHAPTER 9

Since the date of my birthday always fell after the excitement of Halloween and before school let out for the Thanksgiving holidays, it seemed the only people who ever remembered - other than Mama, were my teachers. Of course, a dusty birthday chart hanging somewhere in the classroom was to thank for teachers remembering.

Every year, the routine was pretty much the same. Following morning announcements, the teacher would say something like "I believe someone here has a birthday today." Everyone would look around to see who was blushing. Then, the birthday-person would be called to the front of the room while everyone else half-sang "Happy Birthday". For the rest of the day, the birthday-person would be the one who got to run classroom errands. Even though it wasn't much, it was as close to a birthday party that I was ever likely to get. That is, until my twelfth birthday.

That year, the nicest thing happened when I arrived at school that morning. In fact, I don't think anything has been in the same league as the thrill I got when I spotted the "Man of Steel" peeking out from under my math book that bleak November day.

When I turned around to thank Ryan, he looked the other way. Even though I couldn't see it, I knew there was a wide grin on his face. He loved surprises, but more than that, he liked being the one who did the surprising.

Thinking about that day brought warmth to my damp jail cell. I flung back my blanket and began to dig through the stack of things Mama brought to the jail the evening I was arrested.

Poor Mama. It was bound to have been a shock when several policemen arrived at our house the evening of *that day*. Even so, the flurry of blue uniforms didn't stop Mama from firing questions left-and-right as if she was the one in charge. In her flimsy bathrobe, if she felt overmatched by all the neatly pressed uniforms, she didn't give any indication of it. Of course, looks can be deceiving and maybe Mama and I should have known that night was an omen of all that was to come. There were more of them than us. Always has been, and always will be. Dad doesn't count.

Mama seemed as tall as the officer who took a piece of paper out of his pocked and rattled off a bunch of stuff. Mother appeared to listen but the moment he stopped, Mama asked, "What time will Harley be back? He's got school tomorrow, y'a know."

"Ma'am, it's not likely he'll be back anytime soon and he sure won't be comin' back tonight."

With that, I was yanked out the door, cuffed and put in the back of a police cruiser which smelled faintly of vomit and liquor.

As I twisted around to look out the back

window at Mama, the metal handcuffs around my wrists felt cold and hard. My arms were slung behind my back which made it nearly impossible to sit upright each time the car made a sharp turn.

When our squad car arrived at the station, things got worse.

Immediately, I was led to a small room where I was fingerprinted. As soon as I rubbed my inky fingers across a paper towel, I was told to stand against yet another wall. There, my picture was taken from several different angles. The flash from the camera made it hard to for my eyes to focus for several minutes afterwards.

There, my cuffs weren't removed until I was taken to a small room off the main hallway and I was told to take off my pajamas. At first, I thought they were kidding until an officer screamed, "Are you deaf? Do what you're told and do it fast!"

My hands trembled so badly, I could barely get my clothes off.

The door was closed but there was a window in the door. Anyone could have seen me naked, had they bothered to look through the glass. People walked by but luckily, no looked in or seemed to care.

There I stood… shivering until a different officer came in with some gray and white striped prison clothes and slung them on the table in front of me. He dropped a pair of thin rubber slippers on the floor and kicked them toward me.

They were so big, I didn't have any trouble sliding my feet in them, although I ended up flip-flopping all the way when to a small conference room behind an office led the way. There, two of the officers who had been at my house sat at a table. One of them motioned for me sit down. The other man placed notebook paper and a pencil in front of me.

"Son, this is the time to write it all down," the first man said.

I knew then, everything else... the handcuffs, the droopy stripped clothes, the camera's flashing bulb was nothing compared to writing down the day's events. I could never put into words all that happened at Muddy Creek that horrible, horrible day. There were simply no words for it.

I starred ahead and wondered briefly what to write. Before I could think of the right words to use, Mama burst through the doorway.

Clutching my own pajamas bottoms, toothbrush and a bag of other stuff, Mama told the officers, "Sorry, gentlemen, but there won't be any confession coming your way. Not tonight... and certainly not without consulting Harley's lawyer."

I figured the lawyer-thing was Mama calling their bluff, like when some fool muttered to Mama, "I want to marry you" and then didn't come through with a ring. Those were the times she was quick to slam the front door shut. Which is exactly what one of the officers did after he escorted all of us from the room.

# CHAPTER 10

From the get-go, I wanted to jump up and knock some sense into Ed White, especially when he droned on-and-on about how jealous I was of Ryan and how I'd lured him into the woods – neither of which were true. Well, not exactly.

Worse, Ed White said the same things over-and-over about how I'd run from the scene and didn't try to help Ryan. He even traced my steps on a chart – a bunch of small footsteps going around in circles. Looking at that chart was hard for me to do 'cause that part, well… that part was true.

Another difficult thing was not answering when I heard my name. Every time Ed White barked "Harley Hamilton", I nearly jumped out of my skin. I'd lived my life answering whenever anyone called my name. So, it was hard – really hard, to put my mind elsewhere so that I wouldn't jump up and make an even bigger fool of myself than I already had.

After the first couple days of listening to Ed White, I knew whatever Mama was paying Ray Paul had to be too much. All he did was jot down notes in a legal pad as if *his* life depended on it.

Even the annoying fly must have found a way to escape the drone of the prosecutor's voice, because it had disappeared.

To take my own mind off of all the bad

things being said about me, I searched every day for a different fly or something to divert my attention. Some days it was a line of ants; others, a spider spinning a lacy web. Anything that moved was fair game and caught my attention.

On days when there was nothing to be found, I resorted to daydreaming. The trick was to act like I was listening to Ed White. Not impossible, but hard-to-do.

Every now and then, someone in the courtroom would cause a diversion. One day it was the hair of a juror. Every time Ed White slapped his hand on a desk or stomped across the room, Juror Number 5 would jerk nervously. So much so, the thin whispy hair on the top of his head would shudder and shake before falling back down flat.

Watching the juror's mousy-colored hair got me to thinking about how Ryan and I used to have a contest during church on Sunday. We'd sit in the back of the sanctuary where everyone in the neighboring pews were sending each other notes, doodling or nodding off. With no one's attention on the two of us, we had free reign.

The object of our game was to ball up small bits of paper and place them in the hair of whoever sat in front of us. Points were scored for the most paper and the amount of time each piece stayed nestled in someone's hair.

It seemed disrespectful now, but at the time, it was really funny. Anyway, it's likely we both benefitted from a lot of good doctrine waiting for someone to cough and bits of paper to snow down.

Thinking of church and "thou shall not kill" made me squirm in my chair. It was one of the commandments you weren't supposed to break.

I missed church. I hadn't been since *that* time. I missed the roaring organ and the deep voices of the men in the choir. I was skinny but when I sang my voice was low and adult-sounding. I liked that.

There was some chaplain that came around the jail every so often, but he didn't sing.

Yes, I missed church and I missed Ryan. Every now and then, I wondered if he was getting a kick out of watching my trial from somewhere on high. Knowing him like I did, I doubted it. He was probably mad as a hornet he was gone. I know I would be.

For a brief second or two, I thought I heard Ryan answer, "I'm not mad." But in an instant, I realized it was only the squeaky floorboards as Ed White walked over to stand in front of two jurors who looked like they could barely stay awake.

"No, it doesn't take a divine presence to see where the trail leads, does it?" Ed White boomed as he began pacing back-and-forth in front of the jury again.

As if joined together as one, all twelve

jurors nodded in agreement.

"The trail begins in a bedroom closet. And from there it leads through Joe Dempsy's yard, out past the Moore's and Stewart's until it ends in blood at the bottom of Muddy Creek. And I don't mean a trickle of blood. People, I mean a BLOODBATH - the likes of which haven't been seen here in Dallas, before or since - thank heavens!"

Ed White had punctuated "bedroom closet", "Joe Dempsy's yard", and "out past the Moore's and Stewart's" with several loud slaps of his hand on a rail in front of the jurors.

With each slap, Juror Number Five's hair flew up. Worse, it barely had time to settle back down before it flew up again. A small giggle escaped my lips. Ray Paul gripped my arm and dug in his fingers.

Of course, the pain of Ray Paul's fingernails jabbed in my arm was nothing compared to the ache in my heart.

# CHAPTER 11

Even though I pretended not to care, I hated not being over at middle school with the rest of my friends.

Ryan and I had been looking forward to seventh grade. In fact, we'd already been to see the baseball coach over at the high school where his cousin Luke played baseball.

It wasn't anything formal. Ryan just headed there one day after school, and I tagged along. As we walked across the wooden gymnasium floor, Ryan spotted Luke lifting weighs in a far corner. After a few last impressive lifts, Luke walked us across the room past a lot of sports equipment and into a small closet-like room. There, behind a beaten-up old desk, sat Ryan's coach.

"Coach Holliday, I'd like for you to meet my cousin... and his friend," Luke said as he threw a towel over his shoulder. "This is my cousin Ryan Thompson and... and..."

"Harley Hamilton, sir," I said with a grin.

"Nice to meet you both." The coach stood and picked up a couple of bats from the floor. He placed them in a bag with some others before continuing, "Ryan, Luke tells me you're a ball player like him. What position do you play?"

"I'm a pitcher over at the middle school," Ryan answered.

"That's great. We sure could use a relief

pitcher here in a couple of years when the one we have now graduates. You could move up in his place, providing of course, you're able to handle the job. Gotta pitch fast and hard. And you gotta keep up the grades."

"Shouldn't be a problem, sir. I'm making all A's now," Ryan answered.

"Have Luke bring you to a practice sometime and we'll see what you've got."

"Yes, sir."

"And Harley, is it?

I nodded.

"Want us to count you in for try-outs or something on down the road?" the coach asked, as he slung the bag of bats over his shoulder and motioned for us to walk along with him. "Well, what about it, son?"

"No, sir. Not me. Thank you, though."

On the way home, Ryan said, "Harley, you're beaming. What gives?"

"Nothin' much."

"Come on. I know you. What's going through that weird head of yours?"

"Well, not that I'm what the coach is looking for, but it sure was nice to be asked," I answered with a playful jab to Ryan's shoulder.

"It would take some practice, that's for sure, but who knows? You might just be the next Babe Ruth," Ryan said, punching my shoulder right back.

"Funny... very funny, Ryan," I said as I

took off running toward home.

I started to tell Mama about meeting the coach over dinner that evening, but decided against it. I would have liked to play on a team but I knew it took more than ability. It took money.

Ryan was always involved in one fund-raiser or another, which was fine for him because if things didn't sell, his parents footed the bill.

In the end, I figured it was safer just to watch from the sidelines than to recklessly dive right in, but it sure would have felt good to be around someone who called me "son".

# CHAPTER 12

Near the end of November, people were talking about Kennedy coming to town along with my trial coming to close. You could feel a shift in the air. You could hear it in Ed White ever-increasing loud voice.

Ray Paul had developed a tic in his right eye and even it seemed to be speeding up.

Long after we got in our opening statement and sometime near the last week of the trial, Ed White took what I considered a cheap shot when Mama was on the stand.

"Isn't it true, Mrs. Hamilton, that your son Harley planned to maliciously shoot and kill Ryan Thompson? And isn't it true, Mrs. Hamilton that you knew about it in advance and yet, decided to keep still?"

"That's a BIG FAT LIE. I told you already. Harley didn't plan on killing a living soul that day. He's not like that," Mama stated.

"A simple "yes" or "no" will do, Mrs. Hamilton. Nothing more."

Ray Paul jumped up. "Objection, your Honor. Badgering the witness."

"Overruled," the judge declared. "Continue."

"Well then, isn't it possible, Mrs. Hamilton, that your son Harley planned to maliciously shoot *and* kill Ryan Thompson? And maybe... just

61

maybe… he didn't let you in on his plans?"

"No, it is not." Mama glared at Ed White.

"Maybe. Maybe not. Let's delve a little closer, shall we? Where were you when Harley stole the gun?"

"You mean when he AND Ryan took the gun," Mama said, her eyes meeting Ed White's dead on.

"Judge… please," Ed White implored.

"Just answer the questions, Mrs. Hamilton… just answer the questions. No additional comments. I know this must be hard for you being the defendant's mother and all, but what we want to do here today is to bring forth the truth," the judge said, twisting his collar.

"Yes, sir. I'm trying. I really am, but I don't think Ed really wants the truth - not really," Mama answered, batting her eyes at the Judge.

"Well, let's move on," the judge said in a kinder-sounding voice.

Ed White cleared his throat, "Yes, let's proceed, shall we? Now, uh…were you home on April 19, 1962?"

"I was at work like usual."

"So, young Harley, over there, was left to his own devices. Is that right?"

"Look, Mr. White, I don't know exactly what you're implying. No… maybe I do. I can honestly say that I've worked all my life and this is the first time something like this has ever happened. Harley is a good kid – the best!"

"Well, I'm sure there's some here that would debate that tidbit, Madam," Ed White answered with a smirk on his lips.

"Objection, your Honor. Honestly," Ray Paul said. This time he didn't even bother to get up.

"Over-ruled. Proceed," the judge stated as he cleaned his glasses on the sleeve of his robe.

Ed White cleared his throat. "Mrs. Hamilton, isn't it possible that Harley planned to kill Ryan from the beginning?"

"You can ask me a *hundred* times, you can ask me a *thousand* times or you can ask me a *million* times but the answer is going to be the same every time. No, he did not! Have you got that Mr. White? Do you need to hear it again?" Mama screamed as she rose from her chair.

"Judge, do something," Ed White yelled, equally as loud.

"I should have you jailed, Mrs. Hamilton for contempt. Do you understand me?"

Mama quit moving, but she didn't answer.

"I'll do it, too. Don't think for a moment, I won't. Now, quit batting those eyes of yours and sit back down. And if you raise your voice like that in here again, you're gone. Got it?"

Mama nodded yes, but there wasn't any batting of eyes now. Her steely ones clearly screamed "NO".

I wanted to shout. I wanted to cheer. But Ray Paul's hand clamped forcefully down on my right thigh and I knew to keep still.

"I think we've all had about enough of this today. Court recessed until tomorrow morning at nine," the judge said as he hit his gravel close to Mama's head.

# CHAPTER 13

"Why don't you get yourself another lawyer? Someone who will sit quietly in the corner while you run this whole thing into the ground? Or better yet... why don't you try the whole case your own way - without a lawyer? You might as well, because you sure don't listen to a word I say," Ray Paul shouted at Mama as he tossed his legal pad into his battered briefcase as soon as Jack Henry walked away.

Even though the three of us were back in the coolness of my cell, beads of sweat began to run down both sides of Mama's face. She dabbed a hankie to her face with one hand and adjusted the top of her peasant blouse a tad lower with the other.

When Mama finally did answer, her tone had softened, "You know I couldn't just sit there while Ed White said those terrible things about Harley. No, indeed. They can make me say Harley shot Ryan... because it's the truth, but they can't make me say he planned the whole thing. I don't believe that, not for one minute. And neither do you, or if'n you do, then say so right now. Because if that's what you really think, I want to hear you say it out loud - once and for all, so I can fire your sorry butt. Do you hear me, Ray Paul? Now's the time to speak up."

"Aw, come on. I don't believe Harley

planned it. But that doesn't alter the fact that there is such a thing as speaking in a civil tongue - especially in a court of law. And I think it would behoove you to remember that."

"Let me tell you something! I'm gonna keep on shoutin' the truth until the day I die. And I don't care whether you... the judge... or all of Dallas likes it one-little-bit... or not," Mama answered in a voice so loud I half-expected Jack Henry to come running back, gun in hand, to see what all the racket was about. Thankfully, the doors at the end of the dimly lit hallway stayed shut.

"Calm down. Now... you know I believe the shooting was an accident, pure and simple. We've just got to find a way to make the jury believe it too. And we will... we will," Ray Paul answered, running a comb through his stringy hair. "Somehow."

"If there was ever a man for the job, it's you, Ray Paul. That's for sure. No one else could do the job you're doing," Mama said in what she and I both called her *fakey-fool-ya* voice.

It was a voice that sounded sugary-sweet but I knew she didn't really mean a word she was saying. I tried not to judge Mama too harshly. There were just some things a single mom needed help doing. No matter whose side you're on, saving a son from a life locked away in the clinker was probably one of them.

Mama was a Pro, with a capital "P". The

more she talked about how she depended on Ray Paul to get us through "deep waters" and "onto the shore at the other side", the more Ray Paul seemed to come alive.

When he took a breath-mint out of his pocket and popped it in his mouth, I knew we had boarded the boat.

Of course, sailing along and reaching the shore were two different things. Mama must have known that too, because she kept right on talking. I had to look away every now-and-then to keep from laughing. Even though I had seen Mama talking-it-up before, it was still embarrassing to watch her rile Ray Paul up.

When Ray Paul moved closer to Mama, I figured he was expecting a whole lot more than he'd ever get and the best he could hope for was a quick kiss on the cheek. He just didn't know it yet.

To keep from thinking about Mama and Ray Paul, I flung myself down on my cot and reached for my Superman comic book. Maybe I couldn't escape listening to Mama practically throw herself at Ray Paul, but I sure didn't have to watch it happen.

As for me, I knew Mama had her reasons and given the option of listening to her ploy or always doing without, I'd take Mama's bag-of-tricks any old day of the week.

Of course, Mama wasn't interested in Ray Paul because I knew her way too well. She always used the same voice when the rent came due and there wasn't a chance of coming up with the money on time, or when our old clunker wouldn't start and we needed a mechanic - free of charge, naturally.

Yes, Mama had mastered the art of illusion. By the time men knew what hit them, she was long gone. They hoped to get one thing, but got another – often a lighter wallet or grease on their hands. Still in all, for some reason, everyone felt pleased. Maybe the flirtation was worth the aggravation. I don't know. This much I do know: I aimed to be a whole lot smarter than the rest of the male population in the Lone Star State when it came to women, that's for sure.

Still, I couldn't help worry that she was in over her head this time. Day after day, most of jury smiled and nodded at Ed White. One lady actually gave him a wave one day. No one waved at Ray Paul, or even threw a smile in his direction – ever. If any of the jurors were moved by any of Mama's antics or tearful testimony on my behalf, they never show it.

Worse yet, Mama wasn't a young chicken anymore. Even I could see the illusions she continued to sprinkle every now-and-then didn't seem to sparkle like they did when I was younger.

I sure hoped our good luck... such as it was, wasn't all used up when Jack Henry shut my cell door as Ray Paul hurried out behind Mama as she sashayed down the hall – as best she could.

# CHAPTER 14

Late one afternoon, I heard unfamiliar footsteps coming my way but kept my eyes glued to my comic book as the cell next to mine was opened and slammed shut. After the guard left, there were mumblings and what sounded like someone giving a couple of hard kicks to the wall separating us. I sensed it was a man by the way he moved about.

Nothing was said between the two of us until after dinner when I shoved my tray of left-over fish sticks and soggy green beans under the bars that formed one wall of my cell.

The male voice next door cleared its throat. "If'n you ain't gonna eat the rest, I'd sure appreciate it if you'd shove that tray over my way."

"Sure," I answered, bending down and giving my tray a hard push sideways.

A couple of seconds later, the corner of the tray disappeared from my sight.

I listened as the metal spoon scraped the plastic tray several times before it went silent. Then, the man's voice said, "Thanks, kid, that was good."

"Sure, no problem," I answered, wondering what the owner of the deep voice looked like.

"Whatcha in here for?"

I paused. The whole time I was in jail, even the times I was pounded by Ray Paul's stream of questions, I never talked about *that* day. I could barely stand to think about it. And I sure wasn't in the mood to pour out my heart to some stranger whose face I couldn't even see.

Silence.

More silence.

*Good grief.* Was he really going to wait for an answer. *Drats!*

I cleared my throat and managed to mumble, "Accident... shot... my friend."

"Accident was it? Well, maybe there's some hope for you then. None for me. No, I pretty much knew when I drove up to my own house that day I was done for," the voice offered.

"What do you mean?"

He continued, "When I saw my old lady's ex-boyfriend's Chevy in the driveway. I knew I wasn't going to turn my car around and drive away. 'Course, if I knew then what I know now, I'd stomped on the gas and taken off in the other direction. Now this. Not likely I'll ever see the light of day."

"Don't you got a window over there. There's one in here - not a big one, but enough of one to know 'bout what time it is by the shadows from the sun," I answered.

"Yeah, there's a window in here alright." The voice coughed a time, or two, before saying "Light of day is what they call a... um... what is it? Oh, yeah, an... expression. Means I won't be living on the outside until I'm much too old to enjoy it.

70

Yes, for all practical purposes, my life ended when my old lady's did. You could say she dug the hole and I jumped in."

"I know what you mean," I answered. A small tear trickled down my face. I was glad the man couldn't see me.

"Thought you said yours was an accident," he said softly.

"It was. But that don't make it any better. My best friend is gone."

"Tough, kid, tough. I don't know a lot, but this much I do – it's a whole lot worse to flip-out and lose control than to get caught-up in an accident. Sounds like you just got tangled-up in something that you weren't planning or there was a big mistake of some kind."

He was right but the big mistake started with my determination to take a gun along in the first place. What was I thinking?

The man continued talking. "And... I can tell you this, you're gonna pay a whole lot more if'n you don't tell it all exactly the way it happened. I don't mean you're gonna pay by just serving time. I mean in your heart and in your conscience. Heck, you're only gonna have one shot to tell what happened. My advice is to get it right. Tell it straight."

I didn't answer. There was nothing to say.

He continued, "Well, enough of this. I'll probably be gone when you wake up in the morning. They're taking me to Angola, a

71

penitentiary all the way over in Louisiana."

Again, not really knowing what to say to that, I merely answered, "Good luck."

He didn't answer and I was glad. I was through talking. It wasn't until the stranger in the cell next to mine was snoring that memories came flooding back.

\*\*\*

*"Whatcha think? Aren't these the biggest worms you ever seen in your life or what," Ryan exclaimed. He laid his shovel next to what used to be the old brick framework of a factory or some kind of building.*

*"Nah, back when my daddy and I were fishing in the Brazos River, outside of Waco, I reckon we dug up the biggest worms I ever did see. Yes, I'm pretty sure those worms were bigger than these," I said stretching out each word.*

*I put my hands on my hips and stared at the worms as if I were really trying to decide which were bigger.*

*Every now and then, I liked to give Ryan a run for his money and this was one of those times. Of course, there wasn't any fishing trip and there weren't any worms - big or small. And the whole "worm-memory" thing was nothin' more than a big fat lie.*

*Ryan stared straight at me for a moment or two "What the heck were you doing in Waco? If memory serves me right, you're from Galveston… not Waco."*

*Ryan picked up a worm that was trying to burrow back down in the damp earth.*

I answered, "Galveston, Waco. Doesn't matter. Everything is bigger and better in Texas. Everyone knows that!"

Ryan nodded.

I continued. "While that's true, these worms were a lot bigger than ordinary Texas worms. Size of pythons."

"Is that so?"

"Pretty much." I answered, trying to look all earnest-and-everything.

"Your whole tale sounds like a big fish tale to me. And you-know-what?"

"What?"

I think you're full of you-know-what," Ryan said, sounding amused.

"Pretty much," I said again, with a laugh, tipping my cowboy hat toward Ryan.

Unfortunately, my hand slipped and my hat fell down, landing on a couple of worms.

I reached for my hat. "Ryan, did I ever tell you about the time my dad and I came upon some worms wearing nothing but teeny-tiny cowboy hats and teeny-tiny jockey straps?"

This brought a hearty laugh from Ryan — me, too.

\*\*\*

The snores in the cell next to mine continued, vaguely reminding me of the lapping water where Ryan and I liked to swim on hot Texas days. Although, remembering wasn't nearly as good as being there, it was comforting to know that Ryan and I had experienced some great things together. Things like shooting hoops, racing bicycles and of course, reeling in fish. Nothing now or in the future could ever beat all of that. I wondered if I would ever again bait a hook or ride my bicycle. Probably not. More than likely, even being outside was over for me.

Jails were nothing more than endless gray – concrete inside and out. Vibrant shades like the green of grass, the blue of the sky and even, the fading pink of summer roses were becoming non-existence in my world except for brief trips from the jail to the courthouse. I missed the colors of nature. I missed the sounds of nature - chirping birds, the croak of an old bullfrog, even the howl of someone's dog left out too long. I missed it, my ordinary life.

I wondered if Ryan was missing the same things here on earth or if heaven was full of the colors and sounds of earth. Was it better than here? Nah. What could possibly be better than dribbling a basketball or crunching leaves as you walk through the woods on a crisp fall day? No, I doubted that heaven could be better than earth. I shut my eyes and reeled in a large trout.

The next morning when I awoke, I realized the man in the next cell was gone. I guess I was too wrapped up in holding onto my dream to hear Jack Henry come for him.

In my dream, Ryan was shaking my shoulder and pointing to a string of fish, saying,

"Throw out another line. We're not done yet."

# CHAPTER 15

"Dagnabit, Harley, you're not giving me much to work with," Ray Paul as he strutted around the same stuffy jail conference room we'd been in-and-out of for weeks now. Apparently, the room had been painted numerous times through the years but it wasn't hard to figure out most of the colors. Dried-up drips of beige, drab green and baby-blue were splattered along the baseboards.

The walls ended up somewhere between a worn-out pink and gray. You'd think they could have painted it something bright, or a happy color, to cheer a person in jail up. Guess it goes without saying no one cares if common criminals are in good spirits or not. Worse, the whole room smelled something like a cross between burnt popcorn and dirty socks.

One of Mama's heels clicked against the leg of the conference table as she pulled out a chair and sat down. "What do you want from him, Ray Paul? For goodness sake, he's just a kid."

"That may be. But through the eyes of the law, that don't make no difference. No difference at all," Ray Paul answered, lowing himself in a chair on the opposite side of the table.

Before Ray Paul had time to start ranting and raving, Mama turned toward me and said, "I know you, Harley. You're hiding something. You need to start talking. We're coming down to the end. It's time to come clean – tell everything. You've got to start talking to Ray Paul so that he can make the jury see that you could never-ever hurt Ryan on purpose."

Normally, I wasn't one to keep secrets. In a way, it would be a relief to unburden myself but deep down, I wanted to take the blame. I didn't want to be saved - not really. The way I saw it, no matter what happened in those last few second, I was the one who deserved to rot in jail. After all, I was the one with the grand scheme of taking a gun into the woods in the first place. *Stupid. So stupid.*

I sure didn't want Mama to know any of that but there was no getting out of giving Ray Paul something. I'd just have to be careful about what I gave-up.

I squared my shoulders before asking, "What exactly do you want to know, Mr. Paul?"

"Now, that's the spirit. I want to know it all, boy, everything... little things, big things. Everything you can remember. Nothin's too little. Nothin's too bit. You talk and I'll decide what's important and what's not," Ray Paul answered, taking a long legal pad out of his slouchy-looking old briefcase.

With a sinking feeling, I swallowed. I wasn't sure I could talk about any of it – even unimportant bits and pieces, without giving away too much. How could I even hope to put the horror of that awful day into words? Even now, none of it made a lot of sense in my own mind. One thing for certain, I wouldn't be able to do it under the glare of Mama and Ray Paul together.

Ray Paul flipped a page in his legal pad, took a pen from his shirt pocket and said, "What about this? Why don't we begin with me doing the asking and you giving the answers?"

I nodded. After all, some of what happened was bound to come out sooner or later. And if I tried - really, really tried, maybe, just maybe... I could talk about the shooting without getting anyone else involved.

I glanced across the table at Ray Paul. For a split second, he looked like a lightweight boxer about to enter the ring. Instantly, I knew from the look in his eyes, he didn't really care whether I was right or wrong. He just wanted to win his case – no matter what.

I looked down at my shoes. I couldn't ignore Ray Paul's presence much longer but I'd have to be careful. "If you want to ask me some questions, then, yeah, that'd be fine, I guess."

Mama got up and walked to the window overlooking the parking lot below. I took a deep breath and nodded for Ray Paul to go ahead.

"Okay, then, why don't we begin with some easy questions. Background information, okay?"

I shrugged.

"Well, okay then, let's get started. Tell me

what you and Ryan talked about when the two of you were hanging out," Ray Paul asked, pen poised in the air.

"Nothin' much. Different stuff."

"What kind of stuff?"

"Sometimes we talked about Wilbee or Tabby Cat, nothing exciting... just stuff." I slumped further down in my chair.

"Whoa, there. Wait a minute. Who in the heck is Wilbee and why did you spend time talking about a cat? What in the world does a dang cat have to do with any of this? Or did the cat follow the two of you to Muddy Creek that day? Is that what you're trying to tell me?"

The more Ray Paul yammered on about a cat, the more I wanted to laugh. Instead, I clamped my hand across my mouth. Right after the shooting, I'd made-up my mind not to ever laugh again. It wouldn't be fair to Ryan for me to be alive and laughing.

Still, the more Ray Paul talked, the harder it got. And without warning, a chuckle escaped.

I dropped my head to the table and felt Mama's arm around my shoulder.

"It's okay, Harley. He... Ryan... won't be mad if you laugh," Mother whispered in my ear.

I wiped the corner of my eye on my sleeve and looked up.

"No, I won't be mad," Ray Paul answered, looking puzzled.

Mother sighed. "Not you, Ray Paul. We're

talking about Ryan."

"Oh, okay." Well, let's get back to the questions. Shall we?"

I was thankful that Mama had done the talking for me and gave her a smile before answering. "Wilbee is my friend Wilbur Cunningham. Tabby Cat is what Ryan and I call Tabatha Clark, a girl... a girl from school."

"Cunningham? The guy that testified's son?

I nodded.

"That's a start. So, the two of you talked about friends. What else?"

"I don't know - stuff." How do you tell someone the kind of nothing that you talk about? This whole thing was going to be even harder than I imagined.

Ray Paul cleared his throat. "What else did you talk about?"

"Baseball, the Dallas Cowboys, fishing... that kind of stuff," I muttered as Ray Paul scribbled across his pad.

Ray Paul's stomach grumbled. This made me realize how much my own stomach hurt, as usual.

Mama must have sensed how low I was feeling because she looked at Ray Paul and said, "Got the picture? There's was no plotting. No big scheme. They were ordinary boys doing ordinary things that all boys do."

"Well, that may be, but I can tell you this. The jury is going to want to hear something more than talk about girls, football and fishin'. And until Harley here, decides to come clean, you're sure not giving me much to work with. In fact, if this were a poker game, I'd be holding one big stinkin' losing hand, wouldn't I? I guess you could say with a dead body laying at Harley's feet, Ed White is holding a royal flush and I've got nothin' but a pair of Jacks."

"What a terrible thing to say," Mama said, her brows furrowed.

"That may be, but I can't see it any other way, and I reckon there's no reason not to be honest with the two of you about our chances," Ray Paul answered.

"I think we're through here," Mama said with her hands on her hips.

At that, Ray Paul flipped his notepad shut, opened the conference room door and yelled, "Guard, we're through here."

Quickly, Mama said, "For Pete's sake, Ray Paul, you're in the conference room, not Harley's cell. You can walk out whenever you like."

Without another word, Ray Paul turned and stomped away.

The fact that Ray Paul didn't get the last word made me uneasy. Ray Paul always got the last word even when it seemed like it was Mama who won. Now wasn't the time for Ray Paul to walk out on us. We were too close to the end for that. Mama must have been thinking it through, too, because the color drained from her face as she gathered up her purse and gave me a quick good-bye hug. She flew out of the room not far behind Ray Paul.

As Jack Henry motioned for me, I heard Mama say "Why don't you come on over to the *Carousel* tonight, Ray Paul? Gonna be a lot of fun."

Ray Paul answered, "You don't say."

"You bet. We're trying out some new toppings on the pizza... pineapple and bacon, imagine that."

"I like pepperoni, but maybe I'll try some pineapple. I'm up for something new."

I watched as Mama looped her arm through Ray Paul's and he shouted back over his shoulder, "Harley, we've still got some things to discuss. You get to thinkin' it over and if'n you got something to tell me, I'm willing to listen."

With that, the two of them went out the metal door at the end of the hallway. I smiled as it slammed shut. So much for dumping me and mom. A couple of beers, the best pizza in all of Dallas, thrown in with some entertainment by some scantily-clad ladies at the *Carousel* would as much as guarantee Ray Paul's improved mood. He'd be back.

That night as I lay in the darkness I thought about Mama, Ray Paul and how strange it would be to have pineapple on your pizza. I wondered who was taking care of Mr. Ruby's dogs and wished it was me.

## CHAPTER 16

A half-giggle-half-sob escaped my clinched teeth when Ray Paul didn't show up the next morning. The pressure of keeping the secret of Muddy Creek must be getting to me. I was happy not to start the day meeting Ray Paul's questioning eyes but if he lost faith in me, would Mama be the next to go? That was the half-sob part. I knew I couldn't bear that.

Thankfully, Mama did come by later in the day. Neither one of us mentioned Ray Paul. If she knew why he didn't show up to question me, she never said so and I didn't ask.

While we were talking, one of the guards walked in and said, "Harley, your trial's been postponed."

"What do you mean - postponed?" Mama asked as she bit her bottom lip.

"Something to do with the prosecutor being called out of town - death in his family. Gonna resume Friday."

"Can they do that? I mean Harley's been here long enough," Mama answered.

"Lady, they can do whatever they want, whenever they want. Haven't you learned that yet? And oh... by the way, Ray Paul took off to go see his daughter in Pittsburg. Said to tell you he'll be back Friday morning."

Friday seemed like a year away but thanks

to a couple of library books Mama pulled out of her purse, at least, I had something to help pass the time.

As I left my cell later that week, I couldn't shake the feeling that something bad was about to happen. I don't know why I felt that way I did. It wasn't the weather. Not foggy or raining or anything like that. In fact, it was a glorious day. Not a cloud in the sky. Still, my stomach was in knots. My clothes felt a whole lot larger and droopier than just a week ago.

A guard escorted me through the back door to the courthouse and we made our way to the second floor and into a rather large conference room across from the courtroom where Ray Paul was waiting for me.

Instead of pacing around the room like Ray Paul often did before court, he was sitting at a table and writing in a legal pad. He did look up or speak which also added to my apprehension.

Since he didn't speak, neither did I.

After long several minutes, I decided I liked it better when Ray Paul was full of questions. At least, that way, I knew what he was thinking.

I pretended to be interested in everything in the room, although I already knew every inch of it by heart, along with the odd odor of it. I wondered if the odor I smelled was fear. Sheer fear. Did the fear come in the room with me or was it left here by those on trial before me? I wanted to ask Ray Paul what he thought the odor was and if he thought it would ever go away, but I'd look stupid if Ray Paul didn't smell anything.

The only thing different in the room was the date on a large calendar on the far side of the wall. I wondered whose job it was to tear off the sheet of the previous day. Whoever did it, did a heck of a good job. It was always right and today was no exception - Friday, November 22, 1963.

Ray Paul never looked up at the calendar - or me. Finally, I decided the best thing to do was strike up a conversation with him.

I cleared my throat to speak just as a deputy stuck his head in the doorway and said, "Time."

Ray Paul stood up and we walked across the hallway, into the courtroom, without saying a word. Once there, we took our seats same as usual.

Several minutes later, Mama tiptoed down the aisle and took her regular place in the row behind me. I turned and smiled at her. She winked back. She smelled faintly of waffles and syrup –a dead giveaway she'd been serving the Early Bird Breakfast Special at the *Lone Star Diner* which sure beat the Tuesday noon one – liver and onions.

As the morning wore on, I couldn't keep my mind off of the weekend and upcoming Thanksgiving break. It was hard to know if it would be better to have the trial over and done with, or to have a really long one with a lot of breaks to stretch it all out. Finally, I decided breaks meant being alone in a jail cell was the same as sitting in the courtroom for fewer days. Both were torture. I wanted to bicycle around town, shoot some hoops and then, go home and lay on my soft bed listening to the radio. Boy howdy, that would be freedom of the best kind.

Earlier that week, Grandma Hamilton mailed some tubes of oil paint and a couple of old canvases to me. The enclosed note said they were compliments of her Sunday School class. Mama said, "More than likely some old fuddy-duddy in Grandma's Sunday School class croaked and someone thought it would better for Grandma to send the paint stuff to you than for it to get thrown in the trash."

I didn't care how I came by all of it. The important thing was - I did.

I could barely wait to start painting but since there were only three pieces of canvas, I'd have to choose my subjects carefully. I definitely wanted to paint dad's motorcycle. Well, at least, the one I remembered. He probably had a new one by now. Even if he did, I reasoned it still might be nice to have a picture of his old chopper just to remember it. Besides, the old chopper was how I remembered Dad.

I planned to paint a picture of one of Mr. Ruby's dogs on the second canvas but wasn't sure which dog since he had so many. I was torn between a shy, timid sandy brown lab or his spunky brown and white Jack Russell terrier. By mid-morning, I'd decided on the terrier. I liked the dog's cocky attitude and the fact that he was full of fun and a dash of mischief. Late at night when things were winding down at the *Carousel*, I'd take him out back and throw an old tennis ball for him to fetch until Mama was ready to leave.

In the beginning, Mama told me to keep him on a leash just in case he tried to bolt. I tried that but after a couple of times of the dog nearly hanging himself, I decided to take off the leash and take chance him running away instead.

The Russell never bolted. Not once. A couple of times Mr. Ruby, himself, came out and the two of us played "Keep Away" with the dog in the shadows of a dim streetlight. Mr. Ruby said I did a good job of catching his fast throw. It was a lot of fun.

The more Mr. Ruby got to know me, the more he seemed to trust me with his dogs. It got so that every now and then, Mr. Ruby would hand me a key to his apartment and have me walk one dog home and bring another one back. It felt good to be trusted but more than anything, it felt good to look like I was out walking my own dog.

Remembering must have brought a smile to my face because Ray Paul pinched my arm, hard.

As I rubbed the red pinched-place on my arm, I tried to focus my mind on other things, like all of the good things my fifth grade teacher was saying on the witness stand about me. Boring, of course, but good to hear.

"Harley, was a valuable class member. Very polite. A well-mannered young man," Mrs. Williams nodded toward the jury and then at me with the same faint teacher-smile I remembered well.

Ed White stood up and flipped through some notes before asking, "Would you say that Harley was a good student?"

"Well... well... I always said that Harley was smart, although he didn't always put his mind to it."

"Ummm... so, what you're saying, Mrs. Williams, is that Harley didn't apply himself. Is that right?" Ed White questioned, all the while keeping his eyes on her face.

"Ah... well... ah, that's not quite what I meant."

Ed White glanced toward the jury. "Okay, well then... let's look at it another way. It sounds like you're saying that Harley could do the work but that he didn't always choose to do the right thing."

"Objection, Your Honor. The Prosecutor is putting words in the witness's mouth," Ray Paul said loudly.

"Objection sustained," the judge said. "Ask your question another way, Counselor."

Ed White smiled. "Fine. I think we've established once and for all that Harley's choices were not always the best. And they weren't, were they, Mrs. Williams?"

Mrs. Williams twisted a flowered hankie back-and-forth. "Well, when you put it that way, I guess not."

Her voice was soft. Even from my seat at the front of the room, I could barely make out her words as she talked on but I didn't need to hear her words now that her eyes wouldn't meet mine.

"No more questions, Your Honor," Ed White boomed with a wide smile.

"Defense?" The judge questioned.

"Yes, one more question, Mrs. Williams," Ray Paul said rising from his chair. "Have you ever known Harley to do the wrong thing? I don't mean leaving work unfinished from one-day-to-the-next or anything like that. I mean the wrong thing - really wrong."

"No, I can't say that I have."

"Thank you, that's all," Ray Paul said as he turned and smiled toward the jury.

"Witness dismissed," the judge said, sounding annoyed.

A couple of next-door-neighbors were called to testify about my character but I didn't pay attention to what they had to say. My mind kept drifting back to the pieces of canvas and tubes of half-used paints. The jury must have noticed that I wasn't paying attention because Ray Paul's pinches were coming at fairly regular intervals now.

The more bruised I became, the more I

knew Ray Paul was getting nervous about the outcome. Even his pinches had taken on a desperate feel to them, like he couldn't snap-back hard enough. It felt like he was mad at me because he was losing the trial. Seemed like it should be the other way around and I should be pinching him for being on the losing end. The problem was I didn't care. Ryan was dead and someone needed to pay for it. It was simple. It should be me - his best friend. It was the last thing I could do for him.

Throughout the trial, Ed White spent a lot of time flipping pages in a really large notepad on an easel in the front of the room. Some pages had maps and diagrams. One page had a miniature outline of Ryan's body face-down in water. There were scribbled measurements on a couple of pages. The best, and the worse, was first last page. It was an enlargement of Ryan's class picture. Every time Ed White flipped back to the beginning of our last school year, I wanted to run up and hug it and say "I'm sorry".

At first, I couldn't tear my eyes away from every page of the large note pad. But after a day or two, Ray Paul seemed to block me from seeing it with his body whenever he could. Mama had said, "You-name-it and Ed White has chart about it, a-mile-high."

If it wasn't on a chart, it was in a brown bag with the word "evidence" stamped in blood red letters across it. I thought those bags might as well have had "guilty" stamped across them, too.

I didn't break-down seeing the empty shell or even the clothes Ryan wore *that* day, but it was really difficult looking at his blood-caked tennis shoes. They were shoes that kicked, jumped and ran ahead of me. Now there they sat – lifeless. I wanted to bawl. I doubted I'd ever know anyone again who fill Ryan's shoes. He was something special. I knew it. Dallas did too.

If only I had fallen sideways a little to the left… or a little to the right… or backwards… or not at all, then fingers wouldn't have landed the wrong way on the gun's trigger and Ryan's shoes would still be kicking, running, jumping - scruffs and all.

Fighting tears and with my stomach in knots, I looked away from the Ryan's shoes and followed the sound of Ray Paul's thumpy old brown ones as we left the courtroom for the lunch break. Mama peeled off down the hallway for the ladies' room and Ray Paul and I went back in the pungent fear smelling room as usual.

Ray Paul unwrapped a homemade pimento cheese sandwich, balled up the wax paper and threw it toward the trash can. It missed, of course.

After a couple of big bites, he muttered, "I can't say I didn't know what I was getting into when I signed on for the job. No, siree. Figured as much."

Not knowing how to answer that, I didn't say anything at all, hoping he'd shut up and wipe away bits of pimento cheese that had fallen on his chin.

Just to be a jerk, I pointed toward his chin to let him know he was wearing part of his sandwich.

After swiping the cheese away, he said, "Harley, you've got to give me somethin'. Fact-of-the-matter, I don't have diddly-squat and we're headin' for the finish line."

"I'm sorry, Mr. Paul, really I am. Not much more to tell." I was weary of having the same conversation over-and-over and wondered what was taking Mama so long.

"We've already had one blow – you being tried as an adult even though you just turned fourteen. This isn't going down pretty. You've got to at least try and save yourself. I don't know how much you know about jail but if you think it's just bad food and isolation, you'd better think again. It's a whole lot more. Being held here in the county jail is a long cry from being sent to prison."

Ray Paul downed the last of his sandwich with a bottle of coke that he pulled out of his lunch bag. "Say something, kid."

"I don't really care. Lock me up and throw away the key, it's all the same to me."

"Look, it doesn't have to end this way. I don't know who you're covering for, but I can tell you this, you've only got one chance to make it right. Understand?"

94

I nodded, wondering briefly if I'd done the right thing. Maybe Ray Paul was right. We were coming down to the end. It was now or never. The real problem was I didn't know which way I wanted things to end. Worse, I wasn't sure I would know the answer to that before my trail ended.

When Mama came back, she looked at me and asked if I was alright. I nodded but didn't offer anything more than that.

Eventually, it was time for court to resume. Since Mama had to work a second shift at the Lone Star, she didn't go back in the courtroom with us.

When Mama wasn't sitting behind me, I missed knowing she was there, although I must admit it was easier to have accusations slung around my head without Mama's low mutterings, which seemed to land with a thud on the back of my neck, at times.

Everything started up again but it didn't take long for Ray Paul to conclude his questioning of a character witness. As the witness stood to leave the stand, a deputy burst through a side door. A hush fell as the deputy's shiny black shoes clicked across the front of the room. Ray Paul was still standing by the witness stand and looked like he was frozen in space. I glanced over at Ed White. He wasn't moving either and his eyes were glued on the deputy, too.

The deputy leaned his mouth to the judge's

95

ear and whispered something.

The judge's face turned white.

The deputy ran back out of the room, leaving an echo of loud clicks behind.

The judge stood up and said, "Court's dismissed for the day! Heck no, it's dismissed for all of next week, too!"

Everyone's mouth flew open. The judge unzipped his black robe and with a couple of bangs of his gavel, he, too, was gone.

Ed White didn't move and neither did Ray Paul.

The audience behind me was silent until a loud voice outside in the hallway shouted "The President's been shot!"

After a stunned second of silence, everyone jumped up and darted out of the courtroom, including Ray Paul and Ed White.

A teary-eyed deputy motioned for me to get up and follow him to the waiting van.

As a brief ray of sunlight hit my face, I looked up to see if the sky was falling.

# CHAPTER 17

When Mama showed up outside my cell a couple of hours later, I sprinted from my cot to reach my fingers between the bars out to hers. If anyone could take my mind off of the sirens that had been blaring around the jail all afternoon, it was her.

A somber-looking Jack Henry unlocked my cell door for her. Mama walked in and wrapped her arms around me. We sank down on my cot. Neither of us said anything for the longest time. Finally, she spoke, "It's so sad, Harley."

"I know Mama. I'm really sorry. If I had it all over to do..."

"What? Why are you sorry? You weren't there when it happened."

For a couple of minutes, I didn't say anything. Had she lost her mind? She had to know I'd been right in the thick of things from beginning-to-end. I'd already told her as much, without the real ending, of course. I wondered briefly if she'd finally gone 'round the bend.

"I was there. Remember? I'm the one who took the gun into the woods that day," I reminded her.

"What woods? He was shot riding in a motorcade over in Dealey Plaza."

"Who got shot in a motor... what?" I asked.

"A motorcade, a long line of cars. Why, Kennedy, of course. They killed him, Harley. They killed him... killed him," she sobbed.

Mama rarely cried about anything.

I put my arm around her shoulder. "I'm sorry."

"Isn't it just awful, Harley? Just awful."

"Are they sure he's dead? It not just something people over at the Lone Star are saying, is it? You know how those truckers get carried away, trying to get your attention and all."

"No, no, it's all over the radio – television, too," she answered, blowing her nose.

"That's terrible. I can't believe it." I took my arm from her shoulder as she reached in her pocket for her handkerchief.

"Well, believe it. It's true. I wouldn't lie to you." Mama blew her nose on a napkin from the diner.

"Of course, you wouldn't lie to me. I just mean... who, who would kill a president? Are you sure it wasn't an accident?" I asked.

"It was no accident, that's for sure. The President and First Lady were riding through downtown Dallas in a big convertible."

"Does Dad know?"

"Yes, he called and said it was all over the news there, too, and most everything is shut down in Galveston, too."

"Are you sure Dad's okay?" I asked, learning closer to Mama.

"Your dad's fine. Why wouldn't he be?"

"I don't know. I just... you know," I mumbled.

"Worry?"

"Yeah, I can't help it."

"I know how you feel. I can't keep from thinking about poor Mrs. Kennedy and those two precious babies. They're all alone now. Reckon they'll have to move out the White House or maybe not. Maybe they'll just let them live there. I don't know. It's all so sad," Mama said, starting to cry all over again.

"Don't cry, Mama."

"It's hard not to, right now, with... you know... everything."

"I know, Mama, but I hate it when you cry. Try not to be sad, okay?"

"I'll try," she answered, blowing her nose again. "But don't count on it."

"Any chance Dad's gonna come see 'bout me?" I asked. My whole body tingled at the thought.

"I'm sure he'd like to come but with his work and all."

"Yeah, sure," I said. The tingling had now come to a dead stop.

He wasn't coming. He probably didn't care that much. Good thing I had the paint to keep my mind off of things – dad and all. "By the way, can you bring me some paper cups? And I need a knife-of-some-kind. Sure would like to have 'em both this afternoon."

"Baby Boy, they're not going to let you have a knife in here. What in the world do you want one for, anyway? Aren't you in enough trouble?"

"I want to mix up some paint colors. My trial's not going to start up again for a week. Seems like a good time to try out the paints from Grandmother Hamilton."

"I've got a shift to do at the Lone Star. After that, I've got to catch up with some stuff around the house. But tell you what, when one of the deputies comes over to the diner for supper today, I'll send stuff back with him. Would some straws do for mixing?"

"Good idea. Are you sure one of the deputies will be eating there today?" I asked, impatient to get started.

"Jack Henry's been coming to eat at the Lone Star since his wife left him. I'll ask him to bring you some straws this evening."

"Thanks mom, you're the best!"

"Harley, it's funny but they've even got the outside doors to the jail locked. You have to knock and wait for someone to let you in. Bet it's something to do with the Kennedy-thing. I don't know. Everything is just awful, awful," she said, starting to cry yet again.

"Ah, you know how lazy all the deputies are. One of 'em probably forgot to unlock the doors when they came on duty this morning."

"I guess. Just seems that everything is turned upside down; policemen and men in dark suits are swarming all over the place."

Mama hugged me for longer than usual, and I hung onto to her longer than usual, too.

Well, I'll be back when I can," Mama said pushing herself up from the side of my cot.

"Mom, where'd they shoot him?"

"I told you. Dealey Plaza." Mama tucked a strand of dark hair behind her ear.

"I mean *where* was he shot? In his heart?"

"No, Harley. A bullet got 'em in the head."

I sucked in my breath. "Oh."

# CHAPTER 18

True to Mama's word, Jack Henry appeared with a handful of paper cups and a wad of straws when he picked up the tray outside my cell that evening. He didn't ask what the straws and cups were for and I didn't offer any explanation.

Now that I had everything I needed, I was reluctant to start painting and spent the better part of the evening sketching out Dad's motorcycle. Since I didn't have paper to waste, I started out with a miniature drawing in the margin of my Superman comic book.

Even though my cell was on the fifth floor, I couldn't see much of anything outside my small window except a small courtyard, but I knew things at the jail were different due to sounds of running footsteps and loud shouting down corridors.

I pushed the shooting of Kennedy from my mind and concentrated on my sketches, trying to decide the angle I liked best. Finally, I decided on a view to the side, a little behind Dad's cycle. It was the view of his bike I remembered the most clearly. Moving away.

After I got the tailpipe just right, I pulled the top piece of canvas out from under my cot.

The nice part, maybe the only nice part, of being locked up, is the fact that you don't have a bedtime. No one cares. The overhead light in my cell automatically shut off around eleven every night but the light out in the hallway never went off and made it handy for moving around in my cell at night.

I shoved aside a couple of school books on my cot and sat down crossed-legged. Placing the canvas across my knees, I took a deep breath and began to sketch the frame of the Dad's old bike. Next, I drew the body. Afterwards, I added a slightly-rounded seat, a couple of mirrors, and the gas tank before moving to the kick plate, spokes and exhaust pipe. The whole time, I thought about the Dad I remembered. The Dad that patted me on the top of my head, the Dad that made me pancakes once and the Dad that came and went wrapped in the roar of a cycle.

When my memories ran out and I felt I'd done all I could. I peered through the bars to catch a glimpse of the big clock at the far end of the hallway and was amazed to see that it almost three in the morning.

Propping the canvas against the concrete wall of the cell, I decided I'd done enough for one day. Besides, I didn't want to go too fast and get the motorcycle done too soon. I had a week and only three pieces of canvas. Mama said that Ray Paul told her, it shouldn't take but a day or two when court met again for things to end.

I never let myself think past the end of the trial. I mean, what was the point? I knew it wasn't likely that I was going home or anything.

Weeks earlier, when we were alone, Ray Paul tried to prepare me for what was likely to come. He'd said, "You know, Harley, no matter what – Ryan's dead and you're goin' to pay."

"I know that." I gnawed on a fingernail, wishing Mama would appear out of nowhere, even thought I knew she was in the middle of her shift.

I hated being alone with Ray Paul. He made me nervous. Deep inside me, I was afraid he might get me to talk. He had that way about him that made a person want to open up and tell him stuff.

Ray Paul continued, "Well, what I'm saying is this, you're in for a heap of trouble. Your fate is riding in the hands of the jury. They need to know *exactly* what happened in the woods that day. Bottom line: the fact is... someone's gonna pay. Unless you start doing the talking, you're the one."

"I understand."

"Hang on there, I'm not through. The thing is… how much you're gonna pay is up to you. You can be a good guy, a smart guy, and play ball with me or you can keep resisting my help and take your chances. Understand?"

"I'm doing the best I can," I snapped back.

"Good. Get mad. That's exactly what I want to see. You need to get good and mad… and then come clean about what happened. How much you pay is up to you. Understand, my friend?"

"No, not really. Ryan and I both walked into the woods that day and I was the only one who came back out. What difference does it make how things happened. I came out and he didn't. That's all anyone needs to know."

"That's where you're wrong. Dead wrong. The jury needs to hear it all... everything... from beginning-to-end. I don't know what happened on the bank of Muddy Creek that day, but I do know a couple of things and your story just doesn't add up. On paper, it may. But here in my heart it doesn't. He tapped his chest and looked at me as if waiting for an answer.

I met his gaze but didn't say a word.

He continued, "I know you don't hold me in high regard. Maybe none of Dallas does for that matter. Maybe I'm not the best lawyer around, but this much I know, some things add up and some things don't. The story about losing your grip doesn't... at least not in my book."

"Why not?"

"Because if you lost your grip, you dropped the gun. And if you dropped the gun, you couldn't have shot Ryan?"

"Maybe when I dropped the gun, it hit the ground just right for a bullet to be fired."

Ray Paul seemed to think for a moment. I waited, barely breathing, to see if he was buying my story.

When he spoke, my heart sank. "No good,

Harley."

"Why?"

"Odds of that a million to one."

"So."

Ray Paul flipped a suspender. "When you're ready to talk, I'm ready to listen."

"I've told you all I know, all I can remember," I replied, looking down at my shoes.

"Come on, kid, you told me the story you want me to believe. It's a cock-a-mamie story, at best. I want to know *why* the shooting happened. I want to know *why* you almost slipped. I want to know *why* you lost control of the gun. Most of all, I want to know *who's* finger was on the trigger. Until I have the answers to all of those questions, I can't do the job I've been hired to do."

I felt cornered. "Ed White doesn't seem to think there's anything missing. I don't know why you do."

Ray Paul laughed. "Ed White doesn't know squat."

If the whole conversation hadn't hit so close to home, I would have laughed, too. Instead, I was going over Ray Paul's words in my head and this much was for certain, Ray Paul was not the country heck everyone made him out to be. Hopefully, how smart he was, and how smart I was, would cancel each other out and I wouldn't have to give up the secret of Muddy Creek – now or ever.

# CHAPTER 19

The next morning, I awoke to what had to be every policeman and Texas Ranger in the state outside my cell. Normally, I would have been really nervous and embarrassed for strangers to see me behind bars, but luckily, no one seemed to be paying any attention to me.

I didn't hear anyone in the cell past mine until the metal door clanked open and the policemen and Texas Rangers formed a circle around that person. Then, they all walked away in a clump.

All I got was a glimpse of a nasty-looking gash on a forehead and a corner of a black eye which looked vaguely familiar. I wondered if he was the man who shot Kennedy but I doubted it. What was the chance they'd put a famous criminal in an ordinary jail cell.

Either way, he was gone.

I was hungry and hoped they'd bring me extra pancakes for breakfast since they'd forgotten to give me anything since noon yesterday.

After awhile, I knew breakfast wasn't coming and I'd been forgotten for the second day in a row. Since there wasn't anything I could do about it, I pulled out the bag of paints from under my bed as my stomach growled.

As I fanned out the tubes of paint on my cot, a wave of happiness washed over me. I studied their names and examined dried bits of paint around their lids. I didn't have all of the colors I needed but it looked like several could be mixed together to get me close. What luck!

The body of Dad's cycle had been a dark forest-like green. I began by mixing green and black in a paper cup until I had it just right. Not too dark, not too light. Then, I began painting, stopping only long enough to roll up my sleeves even though it was drafty in my cell.

I would have preferred to paint with various-size small brushes but all I had were the two Grandmother Hamilton had sent – one small and one large.

Chrome. That was going to be a problem. I'd have to settle if I couldn't get the color right since I didn't have any paint that came close to that color. A mixture of gray, white and black would have to do.

To be perfectly honest, Dad's motorcycle was old back when he first bought it. The chrome on his cycle had always been more gray-looking than silver. The cycle wasn't shiny, either. It was a faded green "Indian", not the red Harley he really wanted.

Painting Dad's motorcycle took longer than expected. My brush was wider than the paper cup, so every time I needed more paint on my brush, I had to tip the cup before dipping in one side of the brush. It took longer to paint that way but I didn't care, I had all the time in the world and I wanted to get it right.

When Dad's motorcycle was finally done, I cleaned my brushes and leaned the canvas against the wall at the foot of my bed. Then I lay on my stomach, propped my head on my elbows and studied my work. Dad and his cycle roared through my thoughts.

Mama always said "Maybe there aren't all that many memories, but the two of you packed in a lot of punch whenever you were together".

Even though Ryan had only been gone for a little over a year, it was like that with him, too. I couldn't stop thinking about things we'd done together. The years had gone by jiffy quick, but I was counting on my memories to last a lifetime.

\*\*\*

*"Hey, Harley, ever think about what you want to be?" Ryan blurted out on the way home from school one day.*

*"I don't know, maybe," I answered.*

*"So, whatcha going to be, knucklehead?"*

*"I don't know... maybe... a mechanic like my dad."*

*"Yeah, I can see that. You're good with your hands - building things, and all that."*

*"I guess so," I answered smiling.*

*"You are." Ryan insisted. "Just think about the things you've done."*

*"What, for instance?" I challenged.*

"I don't know. Wait... yes, I do. Remember when Tabby Cat got locked out her house? If we hadn't been passing by at the same time, she'd been out there in the cold for ... a... very... long... time," Ryan said, drawing out his voice like a warped record.

"Shucks, not that hard to pick a lock," I answered with a laugh.

"No? But that's the point. You were the one who could do it. Not Tabby. Not me. It was you... and... your... magical... nimble... fingers," Ryan answered, still warping his voice in slow motion.

"You're so full of it. And anyway, I don't know if I really want to be a mechanic or not," I answered, jumping over a puddle of muddy water.

Even though it had been raining for most of the day, we weren't in any hurry to get home. Luckily, we still had a couple of blocks to go before parting at the corner of Elm and Pine.

"Hey, Ryan, what do you want to be? It's your turn. Better make it good."

"Me? I don't know. Can't picture it. Nothin' much comes to mind."

"Well, you've got to be something, so pick," I urged, curious to hear what he had to say.

We walked on in silence until he finally said, "Hey, I know, maybe a bird, a plane... something up in the sky!"

"It's Superman, that's you, Ryan,"

"Yeah, sure, whatever you say," Ryan answered as he stomped in rainwater that lay in a dip on the sidewalk, splashing water all over me. Himself, too.

*At that point, I took off running. I ran as fast as I could, but I was no match for the likes of Ryan. In no time at all, instead of tackling me as I expected, he sprinted past, yelling "You can't catch me. I'm the Gingerbread Man. Run, run, run as fast as you can. You can't catch me, I'm the Gingerbread Man."*

*At the sound of something so childish, I burst out laughing and fell even further behind.*

*I expected to find him waiting beneath the street sign at Elm and Pine. Once I got there, I was extremely disappointed to find out that he had gone on ahead.*

\*\*\*

"Wake up, Harley, you've got a visitor," some new deputy said with a shake of my shoulder.

"Are we having gingerbread today," I answered, groggily smacking my lips.

"What? No, get up. You've got a visitor. Says he's a friend. Do you want to see him or not?"

"Send Ryan on back," I said, rubbing my eyes and sliding my feet over the edge of my cot.

"Ryan? You punk! I ought to report this to the judge. You little hood. Or better yet, I ought to wallop your bottom, right here and now. Do I make myself understood?"

"Sorry. I must have been dreaming."

"You twerpy kid."

"I said I'm sorry. Anyway, who's here to

see me? No one comes to see me," I asked, still struggling to come to my senses.

"Says he's a buddy... Wilbur Cunningham. Know him?"

I nodded.

"Why he'd bother to fight all the news reporters and Kennedy looky-loos to see you beats me."

I nodded again. "I know him. Give me a minute to... you know what," I said, turning toward the wide-open toilet. I unzipped my pants.

"Okay, but only for Wilbur's sake."

"Yeah, sure. Thanks," I answered as the deputy strutted away.

I barely had time to zip-up my pants before the deputy walked back toward my cell with Wilbur following close behind.

My face felt flushed. I was excited to have a visitor but other than Mama and Ray Paul, no one had seen me behind bars. At first, I looked down at the floor but since there wasn't anything I could do about him seeing me locked up, I lifted my head until my eyes met his.

After the deputy unlocked the door, Wilbur stepped in.

"Hey, Harley," Wilbur said, thrusting his hands in his pockets.

"Hey, Wilbur," I answered.

"How are you doing in here?"

"Okay, I guess. Here... have a seat." I answered, motioning for him to sit down on my cot.

He stayed standing. "Thanks. What you been doing?"

"Nothing much."

"Whatcha been painting there?" he asked, looking at my canvas of Dad's motorcycle.

"My dad's old Indian motorcycle. Had it when I was born. He's probably got a red Harley by now. This is just the one I remember from a long time ago."

"It's good," he answered.

"It's okay."

"Whatcha going to do with it?"

"Ah, I don't know. Keep it, I guess. Just something to have around," I replied, even though I knew I'd never part with it.

"Well, guess I'd better go. I only came by to say 'hi'."

"Thanks, Wilbur. Thanks for coming."

"No problem," he answered, waving for the deputy at the far end of the hall.

"Hey, Wilbur, tell your father something for me."

"Sure… what?"

"Tell him I said thanks for saying all my dad always paid what he owed. It really meant a lot to hear it."

"I will. Take care, Harley," he answered as he stepped through the doorway.

I thought he was through talking, but all of a sudden, he turned and looked back at me.

114

Through the bars, he asked, "Do you miss him?"

"Every second of the day."

"Well, then, that's enough for me."

"Bye," I replied.

It didn't matter if Wilbur was talking about Dad or Ryan. My answer would have been the same.

# CHAPTER 20

Thinking about Wilbur's visit made me smile. I missed hanging out with other kids and wondered if Wilbur would come back. I hoped so, but doubted he would. We'd probably said all there was to say.

When Mama showed up at the jail later that morning, I told her about Wilbur's visit. Not exactly what we said, but the fact that he came. She seemed mighty pleased and said that a lot of people in Dallas were rooting for me. To hear her tell it, it was as if everyone over at the Lone Star Diner had placed their bets and a lot of money was riding on me being found innocent. I doubted that, but it felt mighty good to hear.

Mama said that a policeman named Tippett got shot by the Kennedy killer and an arrest had been made. She said they'd put a television on the counter in the Lone Star for everyone to watch the news while they ate. I wondered if I should be worried about her. She was dressed in nothing but black from head-to-toe, except for her white work apron, which had the words "Lone Star Diner" stitched in blood red across it.

Even though I couldn't put my finger on it, Mama didn't look the same. Of course, neither did I. I'd changed since *Muddy Creek*. I was only twelve... twelve and three-fourths, when *it* happened and that was well over a year ago.

Mama always worked long shifts and never had any time for herself. Mama's shoulders were stooped and she yawned constantly, so she must not be sleeping much, probably some of it on account of worrying about me. Some it on account of the Kennedy stuff.

"Mama, don't worry about coming here to see me. I'm going to be busy. I've got an idea for my next painting," I remarked over a couple of pieces of left-over pizza Mama brought from the Carousel. I didn't tell her the jail had stop feeding me since Kennedy. It would rile her up more than she was already.

"What are you fixin' to paint this time, Harley? I hope it's not anything more to do with your dad."

"No. I've been thinking about painting one of Jack Ruby's dogs, the one that likes to play ball."

"Sounds nice."

"Yeah, I think so, too, if I've got enough black and white left-over from painting Dad's cycle," I replied.

"Harley, I've got a great idea. Did you know President Johnson calls his wife "Ladybug. No, wait... maybe its Ladybird.""

"He does? That's silly."

"Well, anyway, why don't you throw a couple of ladybugs in your picture - like a tribute or something?"

"Ummm... I uh... I uh guess I could," I

answered, thinking the whole Kennedy thing, on top of *my* trial, had really taken her over the top.

I expected Mama to call for the guard to let her out but she sat still, starring at her hands.

"What's wrong, Mama?"

"I've been trying to decide whether to tell you something or not, but the more I think about it, the more I think I should."

Small beads of sweat broke out on my forehead. "What?"

"Well, ummm... the man... the man who shot Kennedy, this man, Lee Harvey Oswald, well, ummm... that's the Lee we know from the Carousel. The same Lee that comes to see Jack Ruby. They're keeping him here at the jail," she answered.

Ah, so that's why the black-eye and top of man's head looked familiar. Before I could tell her I thought I'd already seen him, she continued, "Now, don't worry, I've told them all out front, Jack Henry included, if they let anything... anything at all... happen to you, they're gonna have to face me. So, you should be safe. Okay?"

"Well, that explains no dinner last night or anything today," I answered, trying to be funny.

"Do you mean to tell me, they're not feeding you?"

"Just kidding," I lied. "Anyway, you know how they are around here – they're on top of everything," I answered in hopes of talking louder than my growling stomach.

"There's something else you should know. The man that killed the president..."

I shivered. "Lee?"

"Yeah, well... he's really bad."

"What do you mean... really bad?"

"He's a communist."

I didn't know what to say to that. I couldn't imagine the small man who quietly slid in-and-out of the Carousel every so often was a communist who killed the president. It just didn't fit. "Are you sure, Mama? Are you really sure?" Lee seemed kind. He always said *"hey kid"* to me... usually with a smile.

"I'm sure." Mama nodded. "He's also a coward. He ran and hid in the Texas Theatre after killing an innocent policeman. He's been kickin' and screamin' on the news that he was set-up. Wouldn't even admit it was him that killed the president."

I didn't know what to say to that, so I said nothing.

A few minutes later, when Mama called for the guard to open my cell door so she could leave, I kept busy, fluffing my pillow.

For the first time in a long time, I wanted to bury my head in my pillow cry. I wanted to cry because my actions had worried my mama. I wanted to cry for Ryan and his mom and for Billy, Ryan's younger brother. And for some strange reason, I wanted not only to cry for the Kennedys but also for Lee Oswald, who had picked up a shotgun and ruined the lives of just about everyone… his own, too. One shot. That's all. I should know better than anyone.

Sometime later, I slid down on the concrete floor and pulled another piece of canvas from beneath my bed and laid it carefully on my cot.

Then, I dug through the paper bag for a paper cup, the straws and my paints. When they were spread out on the cot before me, I was ready to go at it once more. I was glad that I'd chosen to paint one of Mr. Ruby's dogs. Animals and nature always had a calming effect on me. Maybe if I tried, I'd find some place to toss in a tiny ladybug. Heck, I'd toss in a dozen if it would please Mama.

First, I needed to sketch.

Once again, I used the margins in my Superman comic book.

Afterwards, with the canvas on my knees, I sat on the edge of my cot and began to draw.

It wasn't easy to balance a large piece of canvas on my knobby knees but I did my best. I wished I could spread things out on the wooden table in the deputies' break room. But I knew better than to ask. They didn't let criminals do much of anything. Certainly, not that.

Most of the time, instead of taking me to the visiting area, the deputies usually just showed Mama and Ray Paul back to me. I figured it didn't matter and I guess no one else did either because nothing was ever said about it. Of course, that was likely to change now that Lee Oswald was probably the one in the cell past mine. At least, I thought he was. Otherwise, why would someone need to be surrounded by a hundred guards to walk from his cell to the conference room or wherever they took him?

Anyway, I didn't really care one way or the other. What I did care about was getting everything sketched-out exactly the way I wanted it, ladybugs and all.

As daylight faded from my small cell window, I decided it would be better to start painting when I felt fresh in the morning. My trial would start back the Monday after Thanksgiving, less than a week away, and I wondered if I could get the third painting done over the weekend. The more I thought about it, the more I decided it would best to wait. I needed to plan things all out, not rush through it.

The motorcycle and Jack Ruby's dog were both just warm-ups. I wanted the third one to be the best, *the one*. Head and shoulders above the rest.

# CHAPTER 21

It was close to eight before my dinner arrived. To my delight, it came with a can of soda instead of the usual lukewarm carton of milk. It looked like someone opened a can of corn and green beans and dumped them out on my tray, and absentmindedly added a can of soda from the machine.

I slid the tray back under the bars but kept the can of soda, taking small sips to make it last.

After tilting my head back and tapping the side of the can for the last little drop, I crawled in bed and fell asleep.

Sometime later, I was jolted awake. It sounded like the scuff of someone's shoe shoved, or kicked, my metal dinner tray back toward me. I could see the back of a dingy white t-shirt in the midst of several deputies who were now escorting the man back to the cell past mine. It *was* the man I now knew as an evil communist, instead of friendly Lee, Jack Ruby's friend.

I walked to the bars of my cell to peer down the hall at the clock on the wall. Two forty-five. Seemed like a long time to be questioned.

When the others had gone, I could hear the prisoner in the next cell pacing back and forth.

After a couple of minutes, the pacing stopped. "Hey kid, you awake?"

I didn't answer. The once friendly man

scared me know.

In the darkness, he cleared his throat, "Hey kid, you awake?"

I shivered and hesitated before answering. Was Lee an evil communist or a man unfairly blamed for shooting a president? Finally, I squeaked out, "Yeah, I'm awake. How'd you know it was me?"

"Jack told me about your problem... the shooting and all, and as far as I know, you're the only other one being held here."

For a moment, I felt embarrassed that Mr. Ruby knew about me being in jail. Mama must have told him about my situation when she asked for extra hours at the Carousel. Of course, Mr. Ruby knew. Everyone did. I wondered if I got out of here, if Mr. Ruby would trust me to walk his dogs again. I hoped so.

Lee broke my train of thought when he uttered, "Stupid people... they think because they say it's so, then... it *is*. But it's not! I'm being railroaded. I'm a patsy and it was a set-up. I'm part of the good guys. Jack will tell 'em. I'm in the C.I.A. They'll believe him. Mobsters always know *the* score. They have an inside track. It's an outrage that I'm even in here. When the government claims me, I'm gonna sue the pants off of everyone... the whole Dallas Police Department. Heck, the whole state of Texas, too!"

Not knowing what the C.I.A. or who the

Mobsters were, or how to answer any of that, I asked, "Are you a communist from Russia like they say?"

"I lived there once, but I've lived in Mexico and New Orleans, too. I'll tell you one thing, when I'm out of this blasted jail, me, my wife and girls are leaving this country for good. These stupid people, they wouldn't know the truth if they saw it happening in front of their eyes. They wanna think what they think. Know why?"

"No," I answered.

"They don't want to know it!"

He sounded crazy, so I didn't say anything else. But that didn't stop him. He continued, "Come to the edge of your cell. Come as close as you can. I need to tell you something. Something important."

I slid my feet from my cot onto the cold concrete floor. I wondered if I should yell for a guard, all the while inching closer. "Okay, I'm as close as I can get."

"Okay, now this is important. Someone needs to know the truth... and I guess fate picked you, kid."

Oswald began to rant about a conspiracy, about some CIA plot to kill the president, about his job being to put a gun in the depository window and then get the hell out of the way for one of the snipers. He talked about being set-up because now they were blaming him. He talked about Cuba being mad about the Bay of Pigs not going right. He talked so rapidly, it was hard to make much sense out of what he was saying. There was stuff about sharp-shooters on a knoll and Kennedy being caught in a cross-fire. He ended saying, "I was paid to put a gun in the window at the book depository. That's all. Heck, I was drinking a coke in the break room when it happened. I didn't want to be watching what I knew was going to happen. Think about it. How would I have known five weeks ago Kennedy's motorcade route? Only the CIA would have known that back then. The CIA got me the job at the depository so that I could hide a gun in a window overlooking where Kennedy's car would slow down to make the turn. Shucks, the knoll, the wall, the trees – perfect! The time... the place... the window... the grassy knoll... train tracks... the parking lot pick-up... the motorcade turn... open top limo... the depository window... me. Stinkin' coincidence, heck no! It was all planned... but not by me."

Since I didn't know of an answer to that, I muttered, "Oh, okay."

"If you don't believe me, kid, think about this. From the time I downed a coke in the break room and made my way down the street, they'd already put out an APB,."

I interrupted, "What's an APB?"

"All Points Bulletin, it goes out to every cop. It was about me – my height, my weight, my age. It even had my photo on it. Now, doesn't that seem pretty suspicious that in all the chaos of the shooting that every policeman in town suddenly knows my height, my weight, my age, my name – everything about me? How would you know that from just seeing a face in a window?"

Since I wasn't sure if he was telling the truth, I answered in his favor. "You wouldn't."

"No, you wouldn't. That's the point. If you were six stories below, looking up at a person in a window, you'd have a hard time knowing that person's height from down there. You'd only know there was a face in the window. See what I'm saying kid, it was a set-up from the beginning. I was supposed to be the decoy, the patsy."

"Why you?" I asked.

"They knew I learned how to shoot in the Marines and I lived in Russia for awhile. Reason enough right there for me to be a suspect. Of course, what they're not saying is that the government sent me to Russia in the first place."

"Who sent you to Russia?"

"Why, the U. S. Government. That's who." Lee answered. "Guess this whole thing has been in the works for awhile."

I thought for a couple of minutes. "Why'd you run away after the president was shot?"

"After the shooting, the plan was for me to meet up with my CIA handler at Jack's. I was going to get my money for putting the gun in the depository window. At least, that's what they said. Now I'm not so sure about anything."

127

He paused before adding, "Boy, was I stupid... stupid... stupid!"

I thought for a moment. "What's a handler?"

"The government guy who tells me what to do and when to do it."

"Did he tell you to kill Tippett?" I asked.

"Dang. That wasn't supposed to happen."

"Gotta be sad for his family," I muttered.

"Yeah... but... but... the whole thing was a set-up. I was their patsy. I should have known when my handler gave me a Communist newspaper and told me hold it up in one hand and with my gun in my other hand, all for a photo."

"Why don't you just tell the police what really happened?"

For the first time, Lee sounded sad. "I told them all – the cops and everyone. They don't believe me... or want to believe me. I even said I'd keep my mouth shut if they let me go back to Russia."

*Commie. So, he is a commie.* I wasn't sure if I was listening to the ramblings of a madman or the voice of reason. Either way, I couldn't think of a single word to say.

After several long minutes, Oswald spoke again, "You'll see. They'll see. I'm telling the truth. Maybe not tomorrow, or the next day, or even the day after that, but there will come a day when the whole world will know that I wasn't the one who shot Kennedy. Ruby will step forward. You'll see. You believe me, kid, don't you?"

"I guess so."

"Well, here something you can take to the bank. You know Dealey, kid... Dealey Plaza?"

"Sure," I replied.

"There were some men on the knoll... some very nicely dressed "hobos" and they were shootin', too. And here's another big secret... the president, he ain't the only Kennedy with a target painted on his back."

"Maybe you should tell that to someone in charge, a deputy or someone."

"I've been trying. No one will listen."

"Who would want to kill President Kennedy?" I asked.

Lee let out a low whistle. "Who'd have the most to gain might be a good place to start. Heck, there are plenty. No communist plot. It was an inside job. Our own people. The CIA with some help from the mob. Cuba sent a sniper over, too."

I scratched my head not knowing what to believe. "Want me to tell my mother... or Ray Paul, my lawyer... or Deputy Henry... or someone? Maybe they'll listen to me."

Lee didn't answer and I used the pause in his rant to ask him the question that was haunting me. Why did you stroll out in the open after the Kennedy was shot? Why didn't you hide? Mama told me you were walking in the middle of the day over in the Oak Cliff area. Seems odd to me."

Lee cleared his throat. "I should have waited until things cooled down but I was on my way to get my pay for taking the gun to the depository. My wife and girls need the money."

"Oh," I replied.

"That's enough talking. I'm tired. Besides, it's best if you stay out of all of this, kid. You might just go and get yourself killed. Maybe when you're older, you'll know whether to keep what I'm telling you to yourself, or to scream it to everyone in sight. I guess I just wanted someone to know, it weren't me. I wouldn't have taken it that far. Anyway, I'm gonna make them see what really happened when they question me again in the morning."

"Hope so."

"Yeah… me too."

Silence.

"'Night, kid."

"'Night," I replied, pulling a thin blanket up under my chin.

The next morning, I heard Lee's cell door open and watched as a bunch of deputies walked Lee soundlessly away.

Thirty minutes or so later, Jack Henry brought my breakfast. "Not exactly pancakes this morning."

"Sure not," I answered looking down at a bowl of runny grits.

"Well, it's your choice whether to eat or not," he said, turning to go.

"Wait a minute... please."

Jack Henry turned back toward me. "What's up?"

"The Kennedy shooting... are they sure it was Oswald?"

"You bet. That jerk left his gun at the Book Depository."

I let out breath. "But are you sure it was him that did the shootin'?"

"Look, whatever that creep said to you, forget it. He's evil... and a lunatic!"

Knowing it wasn't any use talking to Jack Henry, I just nodded.

Later that day, I heard what sounded like a loud firecracker, immediately followed by a lot of terrified screams and the sound of running footsteps.

Immediately, the shriek of sirens sounded like a million police cars were about to plow through my cell.

I didn't know what had happened, but I knew it was bound to be bad. Feeling scared, I called out, "Jack Henry, you there? Hello? Anybody?"

No answer.

For the first time since *Muddy*, my legs would no longer hold me up. I slid down to the floor and rolled under my cot, wishing someone would come and tell me what was happening on the other side of the door and yet, dreading to know at the same time.

Soon after, there was a flurry of movement and a pair of well-worn high heels in my line of vision. I slid out from beneath my cot just as Jack Henry unlocked the door to my cell.

"You okay?" Mama asked.

I nodded.

"Stand up, baby. Give me your hand and I'll help you off that dirty floor. Come over here and sit down."

With Mama's help, I pulled myself up and fell on my cot against her, leaning my head on her shoulder for comfort and support.

"It's okay. Everything's okay," Mama cooed.

"What happened?"

"Policemen were leaving here with Lee when someone shot and killed him."

I sucked in my breath.

Mama continued, "And Harley, worse yet, Lee was handcuffed to a policeman, a man meant to protect him."

I thought about that for a moment. "You mean he couldn't run to or hide?"

"No." Mama blew her nose on wadded up tissue."

My heart was beating fast. "Mama, Lee said he didn't do it. He said he was innocent and that he didn't kill Kennedy. What if he was telling the truth? What if it was all a big mistake?"

Mama looked me straight in my eyes. "Then, he paid the ultimate price for something he didn't do which would be really, really sad."

I nodded, looked down, not wanting her to see the tears in my eyes, knowing I was in the same spot.

"I don't want to upset you, Harley, anymore than you obviously are, but you need to know the truth."

I answered "I'm fine" wishing she would go so that I could have a good cry.

"Are you sure?"

"Sure, I'm fine. Aren't I always?"

"Harley, I want you to know that I'll never forgive myself for not being able to post bail back at your bond hearing. I hate that you've had to stay in this stink-hole for months waiting to go to trial, instead of being home where you belong."

I threw my arms around Mama's shoulders. "It's okay. Really it is."

Mama hugged me back. "I downright despise being poor."

I couldn't think of an answer, so I just hugged her tighter and nodded.

When we broke apart, Mama said, "Harley, there's something else I've been dreading to tell you but you need to know the rest of it."

"What's that?"

"It was Jack Ruby that killed Oswald."

My cell was starting to spin around me. Mr. Ruby. The dogs. Impossible!

"Why, Mama, why? Why would Mr. Ruby shoot Lee, his friend?"

A tear slid down Mama's face. "I don't know, Harley. I don't think no one does."

The sky really was falling and I was stuck in jail.

Now, I desperately wanted Mama to leave and yet, I didn't want her to go. What if something happened to her? What if someone shot her? What if someone ran in here and shot me?

I didn't know what Mama was thinking about, but the two of us stayed quiet for the longest time, just sitting side-by-side on the edge of my cot.

A long time later, Mama asked, "Had any lunch yet?"

"I'm not hungry."

"Nonsense. You've got to eat."

I shrugged my shoulders.

"Well, I'll go see about it. Need anything else?"

"No really, except I want to know, where did Officer Tippett get shot?"

Mama looked puzzled before answering, "I told you in the Oak Cliff area."

"But where in the Oak Cliff area?"

"Let me think. Oh, yes, it was close to the corner of 10$^{th}$ and Patton."

Trying not to explode, I raised my voice and said, "But which street were they on?"

"East 10$^{th}$. Now, tell me why you want to know."

I shrugged my shoulder and lied. "No reason, just curious."

Carefully, I slid one of my finished canvases out from under my cot. "Mama, please ask around about what's going to happen to Mr. Ruby's dogs." I pointed to my picture. "Especially the one that looks like this."

Mama merely nodded and called for someone to unlock my cell so that she could go and find me something to eat.

I strained through the bars to watch her walk away, praying nothing would happen to her and she'd come back, lunch or not.


Mama did come back and when she did, she had a peanut butter and jelly sandwich for me. It probably would have tasted better if I hadn't figured out why Lee shot Officer Tippett where he did.

I knew the Oak Cliff area well, very well. I'd walked the same route many times on my way to Mr. Ruby's apartment to let his dogs left out when there was a party or special event at The Carousel. I didn't need a map to know you could draw a straight line from where Officer Tippett was shot to Jack Ruby's. I wonder how long it would take Dallas and the rest of the world to know who Lee was on his way to see.

# CHAPTER 22

Sunday afternoon rolled around quickly. Mama and Ray Paul must have talked together earlier because the two of them showed up outside my cell together. Both stared straight at me for a second or two before Ray Paul called for someone to open my cell door.

Neither said a word until an unfamiliar guard appeared.

As the guard fumbled with his keys, Ray Paul said, "I want the three of us to move to an interrogation room. I'm tired of being scrunched up in that small cell trying to sort things out."

"No, problem," the guard answered as he unlocked the door and gave Mama a wink which she didn't return.

I wanted to deck the son-of-a-gun but the business of moving to an interrogation room made me uneasy. Was this the same room where Lee was questioned?

Mama was unusually quiet until we got settled. "Harley, there's something we need to discuss."

"What's that?"

"You remember what I told you about Lee Oswald?"

I nodded

"In front of the television cameras, he just kept saying that he was a patsy."

"Did he say anything about the CIA, the Mob, or Cuba?" I questioned.

"Heavens no," she answered. "Why would he say that?"

Ray Paul ran a hand through his shaggy yellow hair.

"I don't know," I lied, worrying I'd already said too much.

Hoping to throw Mama off, I asked, "What's a patsy?"

Before Mama had a chance to answer, Ray Paul butted in, "That's a person who takes the blame for someone else. Now, just think about it. Here he is, he may have taken the blame for someone else and now... look... Oswald is gone... gone for good."

When I didn't say anything, he continued talking, "Not a pretty picture, is it?"

"I guess not, but I don't see what any of this has to do with me. I mean, I'm sorry the president got shot and those two little kids lost their daddy. But I don't see what any of this has to do with me." Sweat had begun to puddle under my armpits. I wondered if Ray Paul noticed and if so, would he take that as a sign that he was about to break me. I tried to steady my nerves and resolved to keep my mouth shut and the truth in, as best I could. I had too many problems of my own to get involved in the Kennedy-Oswald thing at the moment.

Even though I did know how it all related to me, I played dumb. I remembered every word Lee spoke that night. It was a conversation I could repeat word-for-word. Not now, maybe later. It was still too real, too troubling.

Ray Paul slung his jacket to the other end of the table. "Now's the time for you to start thinking straight. Have I made myself clear?"

As always, Mama stepped in. "Not so hard, Ray Paul."

Mama turned and looked at me. "Harley, we've given you every chance to tell the whole truth. Not bits and piece – all of it. I know you. I know when you're being truthful and I know when you're lying. I also know when you're hiding something from me. And right now, I know you're hiding the most important thing in your entire life. Am I right?"

I wanted to nod but I stared straight ahead. I wanted to spill my guts about Oswald… and Ryan, but I couldn't. Besides, they were only talking about Ryan. Keeping the secret of Muddy Creek was the last, very last thing I could do for him. More than anybody, I knew how much he loved his little brother. If I lived to be a hundred, I didn't plan to tell the Secret of Muddy Creek to another living soul.

"Harley, I want you to listen and listen well," Mama continued.

"Okay."

"I know you are a good-hearted, loyal person. Maybe the most loyal person I've ever known in my life. But maybe you're not the best judge of what or what not to tell. Why don't we weigh all of the pros and cons together? Just the three of us."

"There's nothing to tell – nothin I haven't told already," I answered.

"Harley, both you and I know that's not true."

"Sure, it is," I lied, without meeting her eyes.

"Let me say this, I've trusted you all of my life. And I have no choice but to trust you now, which is exactly what I am going to do. Just remember when you're ready to talk. I'm ready to listen - Ray Paul, too."

"Thanks, Mama," I answered. I wanted to jump up and hug her. She may not have always been the best mother in the world, but she'd always been the best mother for me.

During our conversation, Ray Paul jumped out of his seat and began pacing around the room, eventually stopping in front of me. His impatience showed with every snap of his ever-present red suspenders. Mama and me, we were in a different mental place altogether. Still, it was evident that Ray Paul was going to give it one last shot.

"Harley, I'm not sure if you know but tomorrow will be our last day to try and convince the jury. After that, other than my closing statement, we won't have another chance to put anyone else's testimony in front of the jury. That means, we're pretty much done. I can't promise you anything. I reckon you're a smart enough boy to know that sometimes they lock you up for life in a murder case... or worse."

Hoping that he was through talking, I started to thank him for all that he'd done, but before I could get the words out, he went on, "In prison, you're facing some pretty nasty stuff... yes indeed... some pretty nasty stuff. Don't think you're not, boy. To top it off, you're young which means you've got a lot of years ahead of you in one of those horrible places. Not like somebody already in their eighties that can stand it for what little life they've got left. Understand?"

"I understand and don't think I'm not grateful, Mr. Paul. Really, I am," I answered, feeling sorry for him. After all, he'd done his best. He just didn't have much to work with - other than a dead body at the end of the barrel of my dad's old shotgun.

"Well, Harley, I've done all that I can. I'll continue fighting right up until the end. Having said that, I need to ask you one last thing. Even though you've made your wishes known, it's my duty to ask you this. Now, I want you to think carefully before you answer." Ray Paul ran his thumbs up and down on the inside of his suspenders. "Do you want to take the witness stand?"

"What do you mean?"

"Normally, defendants don't take the stand, but in your case, I think it would be a good idea for you to tell your side. Tell what happened. Let the jury hear from you. Of course, that would mean you'd be cross-examined. Could get a little tough," he said as he took out a pen.

"I don't guess so," I answered.

"Well, then, let's put your refusal to testify in writing. That way, on down the line, in a few years from now, when you're full of rage at me for not putting you on the stand, I'll have this." Ray Paul shoved a legal document my way. He pointed to a line at the bottom of the page above the word "Signature".

"Doubt I'll change my mind," I answered, taking his pen which felt heavy in my hand.

Quickly, Mama picked up the sheet of paper before I wrote my name. "Why don't we wait until sometime tomorrow to finalize this? What do you say, Ray Paul? Let's head over to the Lone Star. The "Sunday Special" is meatloaf and mashed potatoes. Everyone's favorite."

"Well... ah... okay... I guess. Think it over Harley, think it over," he stated, reaching for his pen and putting it back in his pocket before turning away.

"By the way, Harley, Ryan's brother Billy hasn't been in court for the past couple of days," Mama said as she linked her arm through Ray Paul's.

"So what?" I answered, holding my breath.

"Just thought you'd like to know, that's all. See you later, honey."

Back in my cell, I couldn't quit thinking about what I should do. In fact, I agonized until the wee hours of the morning, but even as sleep enveloped me, I had no idea what I would say or do.

# CHAPTER 23

On trial days, Ray Paul and Mama usually met me at the courthouse, but on Monday morning they showed up at the jail together long before dawn.

"Why aren't we meeting at the courthouse like always?" I asked.-

Ray Paul said, "We need to get over to the courthouse earlier than usual. There was already a line of spectators when I drove by on the way here."

"Great, just great," I muttered.

Ray Paul continued, "Got permission for your mom and me to ride over in the police van with you. That way, we can talk along the way."

"Oh." It was the only thing I could think of to say, although there were a ton of questions zigzagging through my brain.

I hoped I would breathe easier and feel lighter once I made it to the end of the trial but my heart still felt as heavy as the first day.

The three of us climbed in the back of a white van. There were benches on both sides. The driver, a deputy, slid into the driver's seat on the other side of a metal grate. It would have been nice to have had windows in the back so we didn't have to peer out through the grate.

Even though Ray Paul said we'd talk along the way, we didn't. Every so often, Mama let-out a sigh, but that was about it.

I stayed quiet, half-hidden in the shadows as we bounced over pot holes, hoping Ray Paul wouldn't start-up about me testifying again.

I knew the way to the courthouse by heart. Ryan and I had spent countless hours bicycling around town. The only thing the two of us didn't know back when he was alive was that some government buildings have secret entrances.

Before Muddy Creek, I didn't know there was a reason for the narrow stone path from the reserved parking lot that led to several tall shrubs behind the courthouse. Behind one of the shrubs, there was a hidden door for lawyers and deputies who led criminals like me back-and-forth to court.

Today, Ray Paul, Mama and me avoided the crowd as we skirted through that door and into the courthouse. The deputy followed the three of us as we made our way up the back stairs and into a small room across from the courtroom. A few minutes later, Ray Paul popped his suspenders and we walked across the hall and into a packed courtroom.

Whatever the reason for all of the people, the courtroom that had been half-empty during most of my trial was now bursting with activity.

Ray Paul whispered. "People think they're about to hear closing statements but we're not quite there yet."

I figured everyone was hoping to hear that I'd been sentenced to death or shipped to the

146

juvenile facility in Brownsville which was said to be full of hoodlums and thugs. Ray Paul told Mama as long as I wasn't shipped to Angola later on, I might be able to survive.

The judge entered the courtroom and Ray Paul stood up to call our last witness, a waitress from the Lone Star Diner.

As we waited for the courtroom door to open and the waitress to appear, I remembered Ray Paul telling Mama that since there were no witnesses to the crime, the best he could do was to try to show that up until the shooting, I had been a good boy.

If that had been written down somewhere, Mama would probably have penciled in the words "fairly" in front of "good boy" along with everyone who ever knew me. Even when my past teachers had testified, they only used phrases like "full of energy" or "all-boy", they never used the word "bad" so I was hoping that would keep me out of Angola when I got too old for the Brownsville juvenile facility.

After taking an oath to be truthful, the waitress testified that I always showed up to walk my mother home when the evening shift was over.

I thought it was a pity she had to come all the way down here just for that, but Ray Paul seemed pleased.

Afterwards, the judge called an early morning recess and once again, we were back in the small conference room. Neither Ray Paul nor Mama said a word. Still, the two of them were driving me crazy. Mama was biting her nails and Ray Paul kept drumming his fingers on the table.

Finally, I walked to the window and stared at the slow moving traffic below. Nothing I hadn't seen before but it was better than Ray Paul's icy glare and the worried eyes of Mama.

In no time at all, we walked back across the hallway to the courtroom once again. The court recorder was filing her nails and the judge was laughing with Ed White. There were muffled conversations coming from the spectators. We sat down and waited for the jury to enter.

Suddenly, I felt a light nudge on my shoulder. I turned to see why Mama was tapping me but she was turned around talking to someone behind her.

I felt the tap again but before I could sort it all out, the faraway familiar voice said *"You could always talk your way out of anything, Hot Shot. Now, start talking"*.

RYAN. It was Ryan's voice.

Without moving my lips, I answered, "I can't tell on him. You know that".

*"Make them see it was all an accident... an accident... an accident..."*

How can I do that? What can I possibly say? Mere words can't convey the horror of what happened and how it happened.

*"An accident... accident... an accident..."*

"Going to Brownsville don't scare me," I mouthed.

*"An accident... tell it now... tell it today..."*

"Are you sure?" I asked with only my lips and thoughts.

*"Today... now... an accident..."*

My stomach heaved at the thought of what lay ahead. Not jail. That'd be easy compared to what I had to do. Worse, I didn't know if I could find the right words, the right sentences, the right anything. Would anyone understand? Would jurors be able to see it as it happened? Could I make them feel and know what happened? How could I not?

There was no other way out. I had no choice. I tugged on Ray Paul's shirt sleeve.

Ray Paul turned toward me.

I nodded my head.

As if reading my mind, he said, "It may get rough up there."

"Mr. Paul. Let's do this thing before I have time to change my mind."

"Are you positive this is what you want to do?"

"I'd rather be anywhere than here but I got myself into this mess and it's up to me to get myself out. Not off the hook... but to tell it like it really happened. Mainly, I've got to do this to save Billy, too."

"Hot diggity-dog. It's about time, boy," Ray Paul said as he slapped his hand down on the table. "Anything I need to know beforehand?"

"What you don't already know, you'll find out later. Just get me on the stand. Do whatever it takes. Come on. If I wait another minute, I'll chicken-out." I knew this was my one and only shot to make everyone understand what happened at Muddy Creek.

The discussion between Ray Paul and me must have caused more than a few heads to turn because the judge looked at us and barked, "Ray Paul, does the defense wish to rest their case?"

"No, your Honor. It does not. At this time, I'd like to call Harley Ocean Hamilton to the stand."

There was a gasp in the courtroom. Ed White jumped up and said, "Your Honor... honestly, why weren't we told in advance about this? We're not prepared for this."

The judge seemed to consider his words before answering, "It seems to me that what we're really here about is justice. Furthermore, it seems like you - the prosecutor, of all people, would welcome the chance to hear from the defendant - PREPARED or NOT. Besides, I doubt you'll get to redirect any time today, anyway."

When put that way, there wasn't much that Ed White could say. He threw up his hands and sat down. Ray Paul yanked me out of my chair and gave me a small shove toward the witness box.

After placing my hand on the Bible and

promising to tell the truth, I sat down and faced a sea of eyes filled with hatred. Immediately, I regretted my decision. What could I possibly say to make them understand?

I stood up, ready to bolt from everything and everyone.

Ray Paul motioned for me to sit back down.

As soon as I did, he began asking questions. He asked easy things like my age and the age I was when the accident happened. He asked how often I got to see my dad and if I liked living in Dallas. He asked about my hobbies and what I hoped to be one day.

The questions were easy and went fast. And in no time at all, court recessed for lunch.

It was the lull before the storm.

Ray Paul knew it.

I knew it and I suspected all of Dallas knew it, too.

# CHAPTER 24

During the lunch break, Mama kept questioning me about my decision.

Finally, Ray Paul said, "Go get some legal pads, lady."

Mama replied, "Are you crazy, Ray Paul, you've got several in front of you."

"Go, Madam, out-of-here. Every warrior needs to rest before going into battle."

Mama left the room.

I laid my head sideways on the cool conference table and watched as Ray Paul laid his head on the conference table, too.

No talking.

No questions.

Silence.

I closed my eyes and didn't open them again until Mama came back just as it was time for the three of us to file back into the courtroom.

My legs trembled as I climbed back in the witness box.

I swept the hair out of my eyes and looked out at the sea of faces, wishing I could tumble down a rabbit hole and climb out in China.

Years ago, I was a shepherd in a Christmas play at church. The director said if you were ever scared in front of a crowd to imagine everyone in their underwear. I closed my eyes and tried to see people in their underwear. It didn't work. When

I opened them again, everyone was still there – fully clothed.

I was so nervous I wanted to laugh, but I knew better. Ray Paul must have sensed my struggle because he practically ran when he headed my way. "Okay, Harley. I want to take you back to that day in April of '62."

"Okay."

"Now, let's jump to when the shooting happened. We've already heard all that happened up to then. Besides, it's not my intention to bore these good jurors with details that are undisputed… things we already know. Agree?"

"Sure."

"Good." Ray Paul continued, "Now once you and Ryan reached the worn-down footpath on the bank, the one that leads down to the creek, what happened?"

Silence.

Even though it was a scene that invaded my every thought, it was hard to find the right words, the perfect words.

More silence.

*"An accident… an accident…"*

"I was the one leading the way and carrying the gun. Ryan was following close behind me. He had the box of ammunition in one of his hands. Both of us were using our free hand to grab hold of tree branches as we worked our way along the path that leads down to the water.

"Okay. I can picture that. I'm sure the jury

can, too. In other words, you were holding the gun with your left hand and grabbing onto scrappy tree branches with your right hand to make your way to the water below. Correct?"

Ed White jumped up. "Your Honor… leading the witness."

The judge bellowed, "Sustained. Try again."

Ray Paul moved closer to the judge and said, "Your Honor, I'm just trying to paint a picture of the scene for our jurors."

"Sustained," the judge repeated.

Ray Paul took a deep breath. "Okay. Harley, how would you describe the trees?""

Taking my cue from him, I answered, "The trees were scrappy and they were spaced far apart. We always picked that spot because we could squeeze through the brush there."

"Okay. Now, where was the gun again?" Ray Paul questioned.

"In my left hand."

"What hand was Ryan using to hold the ammunition?'

"His left."

"Okay then, so then both of you were using your right hands to hold onto branches, Right?"

I nodded.

Ed White jumped up. "We need a 'yes' or a 'no', Judge."

"Substained," the judge boomed.

Ray Paul smiled. "Are you right-handed?"

I answered, "Yes."

Ray Paul shot the jury another smile as if to say "Isn't Ed White the silliest thing?" before asking, "Was Ryan Thompson right-handed?"

Again, I answered, "Yes."

Ed White was out of his seat lickety-split. "Wouldn't a family member of Ryan Thompson be the one to answer this?"

Looking annoyed, the judged answered, "Overruled."

Ray Paul flash another "Isn't the prosecutor silly?" look toward the jury and asked, "Harley, did you make it all the way down to the water below?"

"No."

"Why not? What happened to keep you from reaching the bottom of the bank?"

*"An accident..."*

This was the moment.

I took a deep breath and searched the crowd until I found Mrs. Thompson's eyes. She dropped her gaze and buried her face in a hankie.

"Harley, we're waiting. What happened?" Ray Paul said softly.

This was the moment. There was no turning back.

I had to tell what happened so that swirls of whispers and guilt weren't forever following *him*. Following Billy.

"Ah... I ... we... ah...."

"Take your time. We can wait." Ray Paul

said, pointing toward a glass of water in front of me. "Water?"

I downed the entire glass of water.

"We didn't reach the creek because a twig snap somewhere behind us."

Ray Paul inched closer to me. "A twig snapped?"

I stalled, wondering if I was doing the right thing.

A deputy refilled my glass from a stainless pitcher of water.

I grabbed the second glass of water and took another drink.

I needed the time to give myself one last opportunity to change my mind.

I looked up at the ceiling where the plaster was ready to fall from all of the cracks.

*"Okay, dude, it's time. Time to tell the truth... nothing but the truth... an accident."*

Ray Paul studied my face for a couple of minutes. "Tell the court exactly what happened after the twig snapped."

The voice of Ryan echoed in my head, pushing me. Tugging at me for the truth. Everything had to come out and this was the day. This was the moment. I had to trust that I had the words and this was what Ryan... not Ray Paul... not Mama... what Ryan would want me to do.

I looked at Ray Paul and said, "I turned around to see who it was. It was... it was... it was..."

My eyes met Mrs. Thompson and I knew she knew. More than likely, she had guessed it from all of the other days of Ryan and me going off to do something before that particular day.

I needed to keep talking before I lost my nerve or changed my mind. I had to make them see that he didn't do it on purpose. It was an accident - pure and simple.

*"Keeping things secret isn't doing him any good."*

Ray Paul moved closer to me and said, "It was who?"

"It was Billy, Ryan's younger brother," I answered without flinching.

A grasp pierced the silence of the courtroom.

My words came out in a rush. "He always followed me and Ryan everywhere we went."

Ray Paul didn't look shocked like everyone else. He just continued talking in the same soft voice, "So, you were in front. Ryan was behind you and Billy was behind the two of you. Is that right?"

I nodded but Ed White didn't jump up.

Ray Paul continued, "Then, what happened, Harley? What happened?"

*"Make them see what happened."*

"Ryan told him to go back home."

"Did Billy go back home?"

I shook my head. "No."

"What did he say?"

"He said he wasn't going to go until he had

158

a turn at firing the gun, same as us."

Ray Paul asked, "What did the two of you answer to that?"

"We told him we were going to shoot fish out of the water and that a moving target would be too hard for him."

"Did he accept that answer and go back home?"

I brushed my hair out of my eyes again before answering. "He said he didn't care and if we didn't let him shoot, he was going to tell his mom and Ryan would be in a lot of trouble."

"Then, did he go back home to tell his mom?"

"No. He grabbed some branches and swung-out to get past Ryan."

Ray Paul seemed to let that sentence settle among the jurors and everyone in the courtroom. "Why would he do that?"

"I guess he was trying to get closer to me."

"Why?"

"I was the one with the gun."

"Go on, what happened next?" Ray Paul asked.

"He darted forward, accidentally kicking Ryan as he moved up beside of me. Ryan lost his footing and toppled into me. He was stumbling forward which knocked me to the side and into Billy who wobbled back toward me."

"And…"

"I tried to keep my hold on the gun but I

fell, losing my grip just as Billy got his balance."

"And when Billy got his balance?"

"His hand was on the gun."

"And when his hand was on the gun..?"

"His fingers must have landed on the trigger because the gun fired and Ryan..."

"And Ryan what?"

"Fell to the water below."

*Make them feel what happened.*

Loud sobs came out from somewhere deep inside me. Eventually, I became aware that my screaming sobs had been joined by other sobs from people around me.

I don't know how long Ray Paul waited. It must have taken a while for all of the sobs to get so low you could only feel them.

At some point, Ray Paul's voice cut through the sadness. "Where were you when the gun went off?"

"I'd fallen on a mossy rock."

"Where was your left hand?"

"On the ground beneath me."

"Who had the gun?"

"Billy... he had hold of the gun."

"Are you telling the truth here today?"

"Yes," I answered, "but it was an accident - pure and simple. An accident. My hand slid away just as Billy's fingers took hold. It was an accident. He loved Ryan. We both did."

Except for a jagged soft sob or two, the courtroom got still. Deadly quiet.

Finally, the judge said, "That's all for the day. Court dismissed. We'll resume at nine tomorrow."

My legs were trembling so badly, I had to hold onto the wooden rail around the witness box to get down. No one moved, except Ray Paul and me. We walked toward the door, away from all the tear-streaked faces.

As Mama, Ray Paul and I made our way down the stairs and out from behind the shrub toward the waiting van, no one said a word. Except for the click of Mama's red high heels, everything was deathly silent. Every now and then, Mama opened her mouth as if to say something, but no words came out until the deputy opened the van doors for us.

Then she said, "Poor, poor, Billy. He's been living with the knowledge he killed his own brother all this time."

Ray Paul made a sound as if in agreement.

I didn't know what to say to that, so I didn't answer. Besides, I was too drained to talk.

Ray Paul answered, "Knowing the Thompsons like I do, they'll have him in counseling before the day is out.

Mama replied, "Yes, I guess. They can afford it. Must be nice to have all that money. Still, I'd rather have my son alive."

Neither Ray Paul nor I answered.

Mama added, "Harley, you did the right thing. You may not know it now but you did."

161

Ray Paul nodded. "Good job, Harley."

We hit a pothole and the van rocked as he continued, "But you can expect Ed White to tear-you-up-one-side and down-the-other tomorrow in court."

The van jerked to a stop and soon I was back in my cell, hoping I'd done the right thing.

# CHAPTER 25

In the courtroom the next morning, Mrs. Thompson was nowhere to be seen. I hated that. I was hoping for a chance to tell her that I was sorry she'd had to hear all that yesterday in front of everyone. I couldn't blame her for not showing up. Now, she wouldn't have anyone to hate or blame. I mean she couldn't very well blame me anymore, and who would want to blame their own son?

With a mean glint in his eyes, Ed White called me to the stand. It was his turn to cross examine me. It was evident from his swagger that he wasn't going to miss out on all the fun. From the moment he stood up, his voice boomed as he paced back and forth in front of the jurors. All of whom seemed to be constantly nodding along with him.

Apparently Juror Number 9 was now using some kind of hair product to keep it from being fly-away because even though he nodded along with the rest of them, every thin strand stayed perfectly still.

Flyaway hair or not, there wasn't anything funny about the questions Ed White was rapidly firing my way.

"Alright, Harley, let's pretend that we all believe the story you told here yesterday. You'd like that, wouldn't you? It would get you off the hook.

"Objection, your honor. Badgering the witness," Ray Paul blurted out.

"Objection sustained," the judge said.

"Okay, let's try again, shall we? Why should we believe the story you told yesterday? Let me remind you that it's the first time any of us have heard your... um.... version. Honestly, can you think of one reason anyone in this courtroom should believe a story we've never heard after all this time? A story we never had any kind of inkling about in the last year-and-half since Ryan was brutally murdered!"

"I didn't want to get Billy in trouble. He's Ryan's little brother. Besides, he was only eight-years-old."

"You mean *was* his little brother, don't you?"

"I guess." I fought not to jump up and punch Ed White in his stomach or smack him up the side of his head.

"Okay, so you're saying that you didn't want to get Ryan's brother in trouble. That is, until you were in trouble and needed someone to take the blame. Is that right?"

"Well, no... uh... yes... no."

"Which way is it? Did you, or did you not, want to get Ryan's brother in trouble once you realized that you were going to rot in jail?"

"It's not like you're making it sound," I replied.

164

"Oh, really? Well, that's how it sounds to me. You never said a word about anyone else being at Muddy that day. Not a word until a mere twenty-four hours ago. Doesn't that seem a bit desperate, even to you?"

"I wanted to keep the secret."

"Oh, you did, did you? Well, maybe... just maybe, the real secret is Ryan's brother wasn't there at all."

Before I could answer, Ray Paul stood up and said, "Your Honor, honestly."

The judge motioned for both Ray Paul and Ed White to approach the bench. Even though my seat in the witness stand was fairly close, I didn't even try to make out their faint whisperings. I'd told the truth. That's all I could do.

After a couple of minutes, Ray Paul turned and strolled back to his seat. Ed White strutted back to stand in front of me.

"Harley, I want you to remember that you are sworn to tell the truth, the whole truth and nothing but the truth. Do you understand that? Do you know... really know... the difference between the truth and a lie?"

"Yes, sir."

"Okay, we'll say that you do. Think carefully before you answer. Did you, or did you not, shoot your best friend, Ryan Thompson?"

"No, I did not."

"Since we're seeking the truth, isn't it a lie

that Billy's hand was on the trigger when Ryan was shot? And isn't it the truth that the gun was in your hand went it went off? Remember you're sworn to tell the truth."

"Everything happened like I told you yesterday. I should have told the truth in the very beginning but I didn't want all of Dallas to whisper and talk about how Billy went and shot his own brother. Ryan loved Billy. Ryan wouldn't want his death to ruin the rest of Billy's life. He wouldn't. I know that he wouldn't."

"Even if the jury buys that and I'm not saying that they will, then why did you run away? Why didn't you go for help? There are tracks back-and-forth from the scene of the crime to Jimmie Pearl's place? It just doesn't make any sense to me. I doubt it makes sense to anyone else, for that matter."

From somewhere deep inside me, I heard Ryan's voice. It was the same voice I heard yesterday.

*"Tell 'em the truth."*

I wanted to tell the truth, but it was the one thing I couldn't figure out myself. It was like a force had propelled me to Jimmie Pearl's house for some reason.

*"Remember… try to remember… remember."*

I wanted to scream "help me" to the voice of Ryan. I wanted to know the reason, too. I wanted to remember. I'd tried a thousand times… in the middle of the night, first thing every morning, quiet times… loud times… all the time I wanted to know. I wanted to remember. I'd never understood the "why" of my actions that awful, awful day. As I stared at the smuggy outline of my footsteps on Ed White's rolling chalk board, their random pattern made no sense to me - no sense what-so-ever. If I didn't know why I did what I did, how would anyone else?

"*Remember.*"

Without warning, a scraped knee, a splinter and a pair of tweezers flashed before me.

"*Remember that time.*"

Yes!

Yes!

Yes!

Finally, the footsteps made sense!

My words came out in a gush. "A couple of years ago, Ryan and I were horsing around at Jimmie Pearl's. We'd made a game of jumping out of the hay-door at the top of her barn down to the hay bales still on the ground. Both of us had already jumped at least a half-dozen times when Ryan landed on an old weathered board half-hidden beneath a bale. Several long splinters tore through his shoulder and leg. I ran to get Jimmie Pearl. She was hoeing weeds in her vegetable garden behind the barn. Without asking any questions, she came to our rescue. Slowly, she pulled out each splinter."

Ed White laughed. "I hardly think that would qualify her to resurrect the dead."

"But don't you see, if she could pull out a bunch of splinters, maybe she could pull out one small bullet."

Although Ed White's mouth was open, there was a long pause, before he said, "Do you know how utterly stupid that sounds… maybe she could pull out one small bullet?"

"It was the only place I knew to go," I answered, knowing how ridiculous that must sound to everyone, but me.

# CHAPTER 26

Somewhere between court being dismissed for the day and the judge handing the case over to the jury, Ray Paul gave a closing statement and Ed White talked about how someone needed to pay for taking Ryan's life.

Ed White said that when it came right down to it, I was the one who had taken the gun into the woods that day. He was right. I was the one. If I lived to be hundred, that one action would be my greatest single regret. I wish I had done anything... anything... other than that.

Back in my cell that afternoon as the jury debated my fate, I sat on my cot and stared at the blank canvas. I wondered if I would ever paint anything again after all of this. I doubted it. It would probably make me too sad.

I didn't get a lot of sleep that night. I tossed and turned, trying to decide on a topic to paint. Finally, I got up and made a list of things. As quickly as I wrote something down, I discarded it. Nothing felt right.

Late at night on the second day of deliberations, a friendly voice jolted me awake. *"Wake up and paint."*

I raised my head.

Flowing from a place deep in my soul, I knew what to paint. I stretched my arm to the floor below. Like the end of broom, my hand swished out all of my paint stuff. I picked up the last piece of canvas and placed it across my cot. I angled it so that the overhead light bulb in the hallway made my shadow fall the other way. Grabbing my pencil, I began. No need to sketch in the margin of my comic book. I knew how to do it, starting at the head. Next, I worked down to his feet and out to his cape. And then, I stopped. For some unknown reason, I couldn't sketch in his face.

I left the face blank as I swirled one of my plastic straws around in the red paint. It reminded me of blood. Before tears rolled from my eyes and ruined the canvas, I forced myself to go on.

First, some blue, which I'd been told stood for loyalty. I wondered if it still did.

A dab of black; deep, dark and sad.

Next, a splash of yellow, like the sun shooing the darkness away.

Lots of red again. This time, the color was more like the shade of a bright poppy, the kind you don't expect to find, but when you do, you're full of happiness. A hue so bright, you break out in a smile just thinking about it.

As the hero on my canvas dried, I mixed dabs of white, pink and brown to get the flesh color I needed to paint his face.

Instinctively, I began to paint the features of Superman's face. Ryan's face.

Huddled among the shadows, amid cups of paint, I could barely see for the tears that filled my eyes as I painted the eyes, the nose, the lips.

When I was done, I dropped the last paper cup to the floor. I had nothing more to give - not a swipe, not a stroke, not a dab.

Stepping back to inspect the outcome, I used my sleeve to wipe my eyes and realized with a jolt, it wasn't Ryan's face starring back at me. It was mine. I'd painted how I felt, not the way I looked. It was me and yet, it wasn't. I looked older, wiser. There was a hint of sadness about my face. It was the look of pain that I doubted could ever be erased.

I laid down my brush. I was done. I'd given my best. I'd protected the brother Ryan dearly loved. I'd given Billy a year of not having to face looks of pity and whispers from those in Dallas - those who were secretly glad they weren't in his place.

I looked toward the hallway light and said "I'm sorry I painted my face. It should have been yours!"

*"You're the real superman... you saved my Billy... from forever living a lie..."*

I looked at the bars of my cell and said, "I'm sorry I lost hold of the gun!"

*"An accident... "*

I looked toward the stars outside my cell window and said, "I'm sorry you lost your life!"

*"It's another kind of life... different... strange... you'll see..."*

"I'm sorry Ryan... for you... and yes, sorry

171

for me."

*"I know… time for us both to leave this place…"*

That night, I found strength and hope scattered among the faceless words.

I found me in the darkness of the cell, just beneath the drying paint. Not the old me. I'd never be that person again, but I'd found the new me. A different… strange… new me. Superman? Hardly.

I watched as the sun transformed the darkness into light, the light of endless possibilities.

In time, I did indeed leave "that" place. It was a place that would never appear on a map or between the pages of an atlas. It was a dark place, a place of grief, and one that tore at my soul but never again brought tears of grief streaming down my face like that particular time and place.

# CHAPTER 27

It's been several years since the jury foreman stood up and said, "We, the jury find Harley Ocean Hamilton *not* guilty on all counts."

Following that, the judge banged down his gavel and said, "Even so, it is within my power to impose a court sanctioned penalty for Obstruction of Justice. You kept your secret way too long, young man, and I hereby sentence you to a year in confinement and one thousand hours of community service. Not that this can in any way bring back Ryan Thompson. What's done is done. I hope this has been a lesson for all concerned parties and even for the people of Dallas who have heard what happened out at Muddy Creek that day. Make THINK BEFORE YOU ACT a way of life, do you understand me, son?"

I nodded.

"Well... okay then... Court dismissed."

I had already spent a full year in the Dallas County jail by the time my trial began so that much was over.

As for community service, I was assigned to a clean-up crew for the city of Dallas and the surrounding area.

\*\*\*

Through the years, I became somewhat of

a celebrity around town - not in a good way.

Once people recognized me, they wanted to know what it was like to be the kid in the cell next to Lee Harvey Oswald. I always said I didn't remember much about it. But, I did, and I still do.

I remember every word Lee said. The way I see it, if Lee Harvey Oswald decides to share his truth with people here on earth, he can lean down and whisper in their ears. If not, his words will go to the grave with me. Since he's no longer here on earth, I doubt he'd care one way or the other, but that's how I'd want it. He knew he was innocent just like I knew I was innocent. Sometimes, it just doesn't matter what everyone else thinks or believes.

For the longest time, I thought I would be haunted by Ryan's face out at Rosehill, the cemetery where he was buried. But I wasn't. When I'm there, I feel a calmness I don't find anywhere else. Billy, who's now close to the age Ryan was when it all happened, says that he feels Ryan's presence when he's fishing down at Muddy Creek at the exact same spot where the three of us said our last good-byes.

Two Saturdays ago, I ran into Mrs. Thompson and Billy at the cemetery. They were planting a rosebush by Ryan's headstone. My dog Ruby and I eased up, our shadows falling across Ryan's grave. As our shadows fell across Ryan's grave, Billy turned and nodded to me. Mrs. Thompson continued shoveling dirt to the side.

Eventually, she dropped to her knees and gently pushed the roots of the rosebush into the Texas soil.

Without thinking, I dropped down on my knees to help her scoop dirt back over the roots of the bush.

Knowing this was my chance to apologize, I said. "Mrs. Thompson, I'm sorry. I'm really, really sorry."

No reply.

"I didn't want you to hear all that in court."

Still, no reply.

"I want you to know that I loved Ryan. He was like a brother to me. I miss him a hundred times a day and I'll never get over being the one who caused his death. You don't have to accept my apology. I wouldn't accept it either, if I were you. Some things are too horrible to be forgiven."

Silence.

I continued, "Maybe I should have kept my mouth shut in court, but somehow it seemed worse to keep it a secret, not only for me, but for Billy, too."

Billy spoke up, "It's true, Mama, it is. I thought I would burst wide-open holding everything in."

Mrs. Thompson patted the dirt around the roses without saying a word.

After several more long moments of silence, Ruby sat down on the ground beside me.

Billy asked, "Is she a Jack Russell?"

"Yes."

Billy reached down and petted Ruby on the top of her head. "What's her name?"

"Ruby. She had a different name when I got her, but I renamed her after someone who loved her."

Mrs. Thompson dusted the dirt from her hands. Then, without warning, she reached over and put a trembling arm around my shoulder.

Billy bent over the two of us and put his arms around us both.

There we sat for the longest time, lost in our memories, clinging together as if that might help us push up from the dirt and face the world.

I wasn't sure if I was forgiven.

The one thing I was sure about was that Ryan would never be forgotten.

\*\*\*

There is a place where I sometimes see Ryan's face. Every now and then, some organization or club will invite me to talk about gun safety, what I did wrong and how '*Acting Without Thinking*' can ruin your life… or worse, someone else's.

Then it happens. Out in the audience, among all those young faces peering back at me, I'll recognize the color of his eyes or the tilt of his chin, and if I listen, I'll hear his voice.

*"Is it a bird?"*

*"A plane?"*

*"No, it's Harley, the real Superman."*

Without moving my lips, I answer, "No, I'm not. I'm anything *but* that."

Not to be denied, the voice speaks again.

*"Only the real Superman would live in jail for over a year to protect my brother."*

"Maybe... I don't know," I answered silently.

*"Hey jerk, you know I'm always right!"*

I smile, wanting to believe I could have been a Superman... maybe.

Another time.

Another place.

# CHAPTER 28

After jail, I tried going back to school but I was different. Too much had happened. Even so, whenever my old classmates get together, they invite me. Sometimes, I go. Sometimes, I don't.

The last time we were all together, Wilbur Cunningham told a story that I found interesting. It seems that one of his Department of Transportation jobs for the city of Dallas is to regularly repaint the spot where Kennedy got shot. Wilbur said there wasn't much to it, really. Basically, his crew stops traffic while he walks out and wipes away oil or grease on a faded white "X" painted in the middle of the street. Using a latex paint, he then repaints the "X". Traffic is then sent around that lane until the paint has time to dry.

The strange part is that afterwards the rag he uses to wipe over the "X" always has a bit of a reddish tint on it, as if there was blood where the paint wore off.

Of course, this couldn't be possible because Kennedy's blood never hit the pavement.

Mama thinks someone regularly drives to work over the "X" in a car that leaks some kind pinkish brake or transmission fluid, or maybe even windshield-washer fluid.

She may be right.

Wilbur doesn't think so.

As for me, I don't know what, if anything, is beneath the paint but I find Wibur's story very interesting.

*Different.*

*Strange.*

# Thoughts from the Author

*Beneath the Paint* is a work of historical fiction. I am not a history scholar. I am a reader. I probe stories on the internet. Occasionally, someone comes along who adds a glimmer of information to what I've already read. Even so, for the most part, I have no inside information that isn't available to the general public.

Throughout the writing of this book, numerous people have asked me who I think is responsible for the death of President Kennedy... Cuba, the CIA, the Mafia, Lyndon Baines Johnson, Lee Harvey Oswald? Here is what I believe:

- Jack Ruby hired Lee Harvey Oswald to hide a gun in School Book Depository.

- Lee Harvey Oswald was on his way to Jack Ruby's apartment for his money when he was stopped by Officer Tippett and panicked.

- Oswald was promised enough money to flee the United States. This is why he left all of the money in his wallet, along with his wedding ring, for his wife Marina to find.

- When Jack Ruby stepped out of the crowd, in the basement of the Dallas Police Station, I think there is a split-second flicker of "thank goodness, you're here" in Oswald's eyes before Ruby shoots him.

  Most crimes come down to three things:
  who had the means,
  who had the motive,
  and who had the opportunity.

It seems like the assassination of President Kennedy may have been a perfect storm or combination of factors and people that is so complex, it will forever shield everyone involved.

## Official Information

A week after President John F. Kennedy was assassinated in Dallas, Texas, on November 22, 1963, his successor, Lyndon Johnson (1908-1973), established a commission to investigate Kennedy's death. After a yearlong investigation, the commission, led by Chief Justice Earl Warren (1891-1974), concluded that alleged gunman Lee Harvey Oswald (1939-1963) had acted alone in assassinating America's 35th president, and that there was no conspiracy, either domestic or international, involved.

## Unofficial Information

Kennedy planned to ditch Vice-President Lyndon Baines Johnson as his running mate in the upcoming election. This, in effect, would ruin LBJ's political career.

Madeleine Duncan Brown, mistress of Lyndon Baines Johnson claims there was a meeting at the Carousel Club the night before the Kennedy assassination. Among the attendees were Jack Ruby, Lee Harvey Oswald and Lyndon Baines Johnson. Upon leaving the Carousel, LBJ said through gritted teeth, "After tomorrow, those SOB's will never embarrass me again – that's no threat – that's a promise".

Madeleine Duncan Brown also claims there was a newspaper clipping of the President's motorcade route at the meeting.

Secret Service Agents who normally walked beside Kennedy's car were ordered to move away from Kennedy's car before the first shot was fired. Although hard-to-find, there is a clip of a secret security agent throwing up his hands in a "what the heck" gesture when this happens.

Immediately following the assassination of Kennedy, government officials fanned out into the crowd and seized over two-hundred cameras and rolls of films. All have disappeared. Nothing has been returned to the original owners.

From the spot where Officer Tippett was shot by Lee Harvey Oswald, you can draw a straight line to the apartment where Jack Ruby was living in November 1963.

War is big business. President Kennedy was ready to pull out of Vietnam. One of President Johnson's first acts as president was to plunge the United States deeper in the Vietnam War.

Lyndon Baines Johnson took the oath of office before the plane carrying President Kennedy's body left Dallas. Photos show him exchanging a wink and a smile with Albert Thomas, the congressman who supposedly lured President Kennedy to Dallas.

On the day Kennedy was assassinated, a meeting was scheduled to place in Washington regarding misappropriation of funds that could have landed Lyndon Baines Johnson in jail.

Lyndon Baines Johnson became the 36th President of the United States.

The meeting never took place.

Made in the USA
Charleston, SC
28 March 2016